$30.00

P9-DEE-534

WITHDRAWN

Maitland

This Large Print Book carries the
Seal of Approval of N.A.V.H.

Maitland

James Patrick Hunt

Thorndike Press • Waterville, Maine

Published in 2005 by arrangement with Tekno Books and Ed Gorman.

Thorndike Press® Large Print Core.

The tree indicium is a trademark of Thorndike Press.

The text of this Large Print edition is unabridged. Other aspects of the book may vary from the original edition.

Set in 16 pt. Plantin by Al Chase.

Printed in the United States on permanent paper.

Library of Congress Cataloging-in-Publication Data

Hunt, James Patrick, 1964–
    Maitland / by James Patrick Hunt.
      p. cm.
    "Thorndike Press large print core" — T.p. verso.
    ISBN 0-7862-7658-4 (lg. print : hc : alk. paper)
    1. Bail bond agents — Fiction.   2. Antique dealers — Fiction.   3. Bounty hunters — Fiction.   4. Chicago (Ill.) — Fiction.   5. Policewomen — Fiction.   6. Large type books. I. Title.
PS3608.U577M35 2005b
  813′.6—dc22   2005005299

For my father

As the Founder/CEO of NAVH, the only national health agency solely devoted to those who, although not totally blind, have an eye disease which could lead to serious visual impairment, I am pleased to recognize Thorndike Press* as one of the leading publishers in the large print field.

Founded in 1954 in San Francisco to prepare large print textbooks for partially seeing children, NAVH became the pioneer and standard setting agency in the preparation of large type.

Today, those publishers who meet our standards carry the prestigious "Seal of Approval" indicating high quality large print. We are delighted that Thorndike Press is one of the publishers whose titles meet these standards. We are also pleased to recognize the significant contribution Thorndike Press is making in this important and growing field.

Lorraine H. Marchi, L.H.D.
Founder/CEO
NAVH

* Thorndike Press encompasses the following imprints: Thorndike, Wheeler, Walker and Large Print Press.

"I think the moment you start counting, you are becoming degenerate. You must think like a criminal, but you do not necessarily learn to behave like them."

—Keith "Trinity" Gardner,
Jamaican police officer

Prologue

There was a sign outside of the Scooters and Hooters bar and grill near Kankakee, Illinois, that said "BIKES ONLY" and if you parked a car there and went inside you would likely find the car keyed when you came back out. Particularly if you parked there on Sunday, the biker's Sabbath. You could complain about it if you wanted, but no one would listen, and if you were lucky eventually someone with your best interest in mind would let you know that there were worse scars to have than one down the side of your Ford Taurus and maybe it was time you went on your way.

On a winter Sunday afternoon the parking lot was filled with motorcycles, mostly Harleys. Riders came and went and the throaty rumble of the Harley Davidson barked in the dry, gray air. Hard-looking men in black jackets and boots stood in the parking lot, smoking cigarettes and cigars and drinking beer from the bottle. There were other bikers inside drinking and talking, some of them watching a football game on television, others playing pool.

There was music in the background — seventies' rock because that's what they liked to hear.

An old Chevy truck wheeled onto the lot and found a spot a respectful distance from the bikes. A yellow Kawasaki dirt bike lay flat in the bed of the pickup. The Chevy's engine cut and a blond-haired man got out and walked toward the bar. He wore jeans, boots and a green Army jacket. A red bandanna covered his head. He walked with long, comfortable strides and he looked and smelled as if he had not bathed in days. His name was Evan Maitland and though he looked like a regular at this place he was not.

Maitland went in the front door, filtered through crowds and found a stool at the bar. He ordered a Miller High-Life, a beer he hated. He took his time drinking it and told himself that he belonged in this place as much as anyone else here. Others saw him but took no interest in him, which was how he wanted it.

After a while he shifted his position on the stool as if the game on television were in a lull and took in the people in the bar, like he was looking to see who was here and if they brought any women that were semi-good looking. Disciplining himself not to look as if he were looking.

Then he found his mark. A big man with a barrel chest and a buffalo's back, holding a cue stick, rolling his shoulders back because he'd just made a good shot and was ready to line up the next one. That's him, Maitland thought. Travis Shelby. Yes, sir. A big boy, probably fifty pounds heavier than Maitland and standing a head taller. The man was with friends too, wearing jackets like Shelby's that said "Satan's Werewolves" on them. Some were as big as Shelby and some were not, but the fact that they weren't big did not mean anything. A short guy can bite your ear off just as well as a big guy so long as he wants it bad enough.

Maitland realized that the safest thing to assume was the friends would fight to protect one of their gang. They might back down to a passel of cops or feds, but not for a bail enforcement agent. They wouldn't back down to a bounty hunter who was all alone and treading on their turf.

The problem was, this was the only place Travis Shelby had turned up. He had not been staying in his home or at the home of any known relatives or girlfriends since he'd jumped bail. And if he left, he would likely leave amongst a pack of werewolves and be impervious to the attack of the outside predator. He had to be taken today.

And it had to be here.

Maitland sipped his beer and thought it out.

In the background, some guys made fun of another guy who just bought a new Fatboy, saying it was a lawyer's bike. Green Bay kicked a field goal and narrowed the Bears' lead to four points. Joe Walsh sang that his Maserati did 185.

Years ago when he had been in the academy, an instructor had told Maitland that the smartest fighter never threw a punch. He might use a two-by-four or a chair or a chokehold, but never a John Wayne roundhouse to some guy's face because that was just the sort of stupid Hollywood bullshit that would get you hurt. If you were lucky enough to actually connect you'd likely break some bones in your hand. The instructor told them that the goal was to *subdue* the turd and eventually put his ass in jail, not win points in a prizefight. He also reminded them to use what they could get away with using. *If you ain't cheatin'*, he said, *you ain't tryin'*.

Maitland got off the barstool, walked past the pool tables and out the front door. He got in the pickup, started and drove out of the parking lot. Drove around the block and then came around to the back of the bar, parking it on a gravel drive. He shut off the ignition and got out of the truck. Then he walked over to a pile of scrap by a Dumpster and picked up a sturdy two-by-four plank. He set it against the back wall of the bar next to the door and left it there. Then he walked back around the bar and went back in the front door.

He did not run, but his walk was quick. He hoped that Travis Shelby had stayed where he was.

It turned out that he had. Maitland went back to the bar. Someone had taken his stool, so he took another one. Sat down and kept a steady eye on the mirror behind the bar.

He only had to wait about twenty minutes. Shelby went to the bathroom then and Maitland followed him in. Maitland stood behind him, like he was next in line. Maitland's right hand hung down behind his rear, holding something. Maitland waited for the man to zip his pants up before he said anything.

Then he said, "Travis?"

Shelby looked at him.

"Yeah," he said, "who the fuck are you?"

Good enough, Maitland thought, and stuck the Taser gun into Travis Shelby's neck, switching it on right as he did it. The shock jolted the man so that he stood as straight as he ever had before falling to the ground. In the next few seconds, Travis Shelby found himself lying on his stomach with his hands cuffed behind his back.

Maitland searched Shelby. He found a buck knife, but no other weapons. He put the buck knife in the pocket of his Army jacket.

Maitland said, "I've got your knife. I'll give it to the jailer when we get to Chicago."

Shelby said, "You put that knife back right now or I'll tear your head off."

Maitland said, "You'll get it back. I'm not a thief."

Shelby turned his head so that his cheek was on the cold bathroom floor.

"Who are you?"

Maitland said, "I work for Charlie Mead, your bail bondsman. You didn't keep your agreement with him."

"Who's that?"

"He's the guy that put up your bond after you were arrested for assault and battery with a deadly weapon." Maitland said, "I see you got a new knife."

"Fuck him," Shelby said. "He took his chances."

"So did you," Maitland said. "Stand up."

"Fuck you too."

Maitland was displaying a cool front. But it wasn't easy. Any minute someone would come through that door and he could be wearing a Satan's Werewolves jacket.

Maitland said, "I'm going to count to three. If you're not on your feet by two, I'm gonna stick this thing up your ass and zap you again."

Maitland switched the Taser on and the sound of little ladyfinger firecrackers crackling blue in the air brought Shelby to his knees, then to his feet.

Travis Shelby presumed they would go out the front and that his boys would swarm on this punk motherfucker and kick the living shit out of him. He could only zap one guy at a time and someone would crack a cue stick over his head and put a stop to that bullshit. Then they would get the keys to these handcuffs and he would get in a few kicks himself. It was a wonderful something to look forward to.

But Maitland pushed him out of the bathroom and before Shelby could say shit he was pushed out the back door to the bar, and like that, the door was shut behind them and they were next to a Chevy truck.

Shelby shouted, "Hey, hey." He watched as the punk wedged a two-by-four up against the door handle. "Hey."

Maitland put him in the truck, started it and very soon Shelby found himself looking out the back window of the cab at Scooters and Hooters fading, then disappearing.

Shelby fought his despair by kicking the dashboard of the truck.

Maitland said, "Hey, don't do that. This truck doesn't belong to me. *Hey.*"

There was something in Maitland's tone that made Shelby stop then. A hollow menace that for a moment made Shelby wonder just how cold this guy could be.

Maitland said, "Buddy, we got forty miles till we reach Chicago. And it's pretty goddam cold outside. Now you're going through a bad time and I'm sorry about that, but you gotta respect the truck. So how about we just drive there in peace?"

A couple of seconds passed and Maitland thought he had made his point. But then Travis Shelby hawked up and spat on Maitland's side of the dashboard. A substantial amount of thick spittle clung to the steering wheel and on the plastic glass over the speedometer. Some of it had landed on Maitland's hand too.

Maitland seemed to study it for a moment. Then he sighed.

They reached Chicago around sunset, the

16

western sky fading from orange to blue behind the dark, rectangular shapes of the city. On I-55, Maitland drove the truck past a man and his wife on their way to a movie. They were in a Suburban so they could see the man in the back of the truck with his hands cuffed to a motorcycle.

The wife said, "That guy must be freezing his prick off."

ONE

The morning after the arrest, they talked about it in shaken, almost hushed tones in the law office where the suspect made his living. It had been on the front page of that morning's *Chicago Tribune*: *Local Attorney Arrested for Statutory Rape*. It was that quiet office time, between eight-thirty and nine, when the coffee's brewing and the phone hasn't started ringing. The legal assistants and the attorneys stood in the reception area and gasped over the scandal.

It was not a law firm, per se, but rather a suite of offices rented by a group of sole practitioners with their individual shingles on the fourth floor of a second-rate building on the northside. Divorce lawyers, personal injury lawyers, trust and estate lawyers, a couple of insurance defense people, criminal defense hacks and the rest, claiming no specialty, merely taking what they could get. Some made a living; others struggled.

Barry McDermott, esquire, did criminal defense. And by all external signs, he had seemed to be doing just fine. He had two

cars, a nice condo in the Bucktown neighborhood.

This morning he was in jail. Arrested on
suspicion of having had sexual intercourse
with a fifteen-year-old girl.

". . . I just can't believe he would do
that. . . ."

". . . I can. . . ."

". . . I knew he liked girls, but I didn't
know he liked *girls*. . . ."

". . . When I saw it on TV last night, I just
about freaked. . . ."

". . . How could he be so damn stupid . . . ?"

". . . Should we really be surprised . . . ?"

". . . I hope he's clean; I really do. . . ."

An attorney who had known Barry for five
years kept quiet throughout most of the discussion. Then he shook his head and said,
"If she's under sixteen, he's going to
prison." Then the attorney walked to his
office, closing the door behind him because
he didn't want to talk about it anymore.

Barry McDermott made bond and was released that day.

The next day he disappeared.

TWO

Maitland had bought the table at an auction at Guthrie's of Ohio. The auction house represented that it was from Bordeaux, France, and that it was built in the 1700s, but only an inexperienced antiques dealer would have taken that at face value, so Maitland had done his own investigation using the weapons of his trade: magnifying glass, measuring tape and magnet. Looking for evidence of repairs, reconstructions and additions. The magnet he used to detect nails. Always, you looked for nails because wire nails were not available until around 1880 and if you found them in the construction, odds are you would not be purchasing an authentic Louis XV period piece but a bunch of old barn boards hammered together in the last decade. Maitland finished his floor inspection, determined it was authentic and set his personal maximum bid at $600.00. It was important to hold onto your internal maximum because if you got emotionally attached to the wares and started impulse buying you wouldn't last long in the antique business. He got it for a little less,

$540.00, insured it and shipped it to his store: Colette's Antiques — Specializing in 17th and 18th Century French and Italian Furnishings, as the sign said.

The shop was in an affluent suburb of Chicago and when he was there, Evan Maitland dressed the part. Pressed shirt, cashmere sweaters, sport coat and slacks. Cleaned up real nice. He was thirty-eight years old and had the lean, athletic look of a retired minor league ballplayer who was probably too lazy to give it his best effort. His blond hair, graying at the temples, was fashionably long, giving him an aristocratic air that was far removed from the actual man that he had been and mostly still was. His face was not an animated one; his expression was calm, but his eyes were alert. Hunter's eyes.

The antique shop had wood floors covered by a few expensive rugs. A musty smell with the faint sound of Gershwin playing on the radio. An atmosphere that made the clientele comfortable in their pretensions.

Like most people successful in the business, Maitland was a bit of a matchmaker. He knew what his customers liked and what they were looking for, sometimes better than they did. So as soon as the table arrived

21

and was unloaded and cleaned, he called
Roberta Sinclair and told her he had a six-
teenth-century French country table that
she could come take a look at. A beautiful,
sturdy piece, he said, solid enough to support a couple of swordfighting Musketeers
slicing off the tops of candlesticks. Roberta
said it sounded interesting and she would
drop by in the late afternoon.

Roberta Sinclair had money. She sold
houses in Evanston and Lake Forest and
made a good living doing it. But she fancied
herself a businesswoman and would not
part with her winnings without a struggle.

"I like the table, Evan," she said. "But I
cannot justify paying thirty-two hundred
dollars for it."

And so began the dance. Maitland was
ready for it. He stood on the opposite side of
the table, shaking his head in disappointment, as if he'd made a mistake in judgment.

"I thought you'd like this."

"I do like it, Evan. But three thousand
dollars."

"Three thousand, two hundred, Roberta.
Don't go to town on me."

"Evan . . ."

Over Roberta's shoulder, Maitland spied
his partner Bianca smiling at him. Bianca

Garibaldi — a tall, slim woman of forty with the elegant beauty of her native Northern Italy. She wore a brown leather skirt, boots, black sweater, and a scarf. Her smile was knowing and warm and pretty; but it was a friend's smile, not a lover's. She was married and Maitland had learned to keep himself in check. Keep going, her smile said, and Maitland feared she would start humming theme music from *The Sting* to make him laugh.

Maitland said, "Roberta, what did you pay for that Range Rover out there? Fifty, sixty thousand?"

"Well . . ."

"In a year, it'll be worth half that. In three years, you'll trade it in." He placed his hand on the table, respecting the furniture. "But this, this will remain. It will become part of the family. Your family. Handed down to the next generation."

". . . It *is* beautiful."

"Look," Maitland said. "I'm not a salesman. I wouldn't know how to do that. I see something nice and solid and classy, I want a customer I value and respect to have it. I'm not going to say something so prosaic as 'I've got ten people waiting to buy it.' I don't, because it just got here. But I do know it won't be here by next week. I just wanted you to have the first look, that's all."

Roberta looked at the table and pictured half-empty bottles of wine and good plates and conversation that didn't revolve around the starting line-up of the Chicago Cubs and what college their neighbor's kid got into.

She said, "Does the price include delivery?"

Maitland made himself sigh again before he closed the deal.

They closed the store at six-thirty and went across the street to the coffee shop to wait for Bianca's husband to pick her up. Maitland drank strong, black coffee while Bianca sipped an espresso. Outside a cold January wind blew a light snow across a row of late-model SUVs.

Bianca waited for Maitland to look up from the newspaper, then said, "I'm not-ah going to say something so prosaic as I've got ten people waiting to buy it because I just-ah got it."

It's not a common thing to hear a beautiful woman impersonate you in an Italian accent. Even when done badly — which it was — it's pleasing to the ear. Bianca, of course, put a stress on the word *prosaic*.

Maitland said, "Hey, I just sell the furniture."

"Prosaic?"

"Give me a break," Maitland said. "It's a good word."

"Do you even know what it means?"

"No, not really. But the important thing is, when you use words like 'prosaic' or 'nuanced' or *'je ne se quoi,'* you do it sparingly. Otherwise, they'll figure out you're sort of full of shit."

"You have no shame."

"No worse than you, my dear. If I remember correctly, it was your idea to name the store Colette's. Though neither one of us is French. But that's the image we're selling, isn't it."

"That's marketing."

"So's 'prosaic.' "

"You are a cynical man. I think that maybe you were a policeman too long."

Maitland said, "Probably." Not because he agreed, but because he did not want to discuss the subject of police with Bianca.

He went back to his paper. But Bianca didn't feel like reading or sitting quietly, so she spoke again.

"Evan?"

"Yeah."

"Do you miss it? Do you miss that life?"

"Nope."

Bianca said, "That's good."

Maitland thought about saying, Why? But left it alone. Bianca had that sort of European, left-wing distaste for American cops that didn't make a whole lot of sense — as if the cops in Italy and France went around quoting Proust all day before kicking some poor bum out of the local bistro. She liked him, he guessed, in spite of his past. He liked her too, probably more than he should, and he saw no need to move the conversation into argument.

He was thinking of something different to say when he saw a familiar face flash through the window, catch his attention and wave. It was Charlie Mead. Bianca saw him look and turned to the door as the man walked in.

"Your buddy's here," she said.

Maitland grunted an acknowledgment and Bianca said, with a note of disapproval, "I leave you to talk business."

She stood.

Maitland said, "How do you know it's business?"

Bianca didn't respond to that. She said nothing to Charlie as he walked up to them. "Ciao."

Charlie Mead looked at her bottom as she walked off and Maitland mentally rolled his eyes. Charlie was Charlie and in the big scheme of things he was probably only less skillful at hiding his lust.

Charlie Mead was a heavy guy, the athletic sort who had played basketball in high school and had been letting himself go ever since. He had thick dark hair and the working-class mustache that he liked to wear in spite of the money he had made. He was in his late forties, the sole owner of Mead Bail Bonds. He had bad table manners and a sharp, perceptive mind. Maitland liked him.

Charlie Mead sat down and said, "Well, you smell better than the last time I saw you."

Maitland said, "Irish Spring frightens the prey."

"You know you're right," Charlie said, pointing a finger. "You don't have a dog, do you?"

"No. I live in the city."

"You can have a dog in the city," Charlie said. "Anyway, you know that if a dog finds a dead animal, say a dead snake, he'll roll over on top of it. Smells unholy afterwards. You ever smell that?"

"No."

"Well, trust me, it's awful. Anyway, do you know why dogs do that?"

"I sure don't, Charlie."

"See, all dogs are descended from wolves. They're all hunters. When a wolf is stalking a deer, he doesn't want the deer to smell him coming. So he'll roll over on another dead animal to cover up his own scent. Works too. I thought of that when I saw you last weekend. Man you smelled bad, I mean bad, but you were only being the wolf."

"Is that right?"

Maitland let Charlie nod for a moment. Then he said, "What's shaking?"

Charlie said, "I got a jumper."

"Yeah?"

"It's a big one. He bonded out for three hundred thousand dollars and disappeared today."

Maitland did the math. Ten percent was thirty thousand. It would be the amount Charlie would pay to bring the guy back or he'd be out the three hundred.

Maitland said, "He put up the bond?"

"Not really," Charlie said. "His ex-wife did, the dumb shit. Maybe you read about it. His name's Barry McDermott. He's a lawyer. Got arrested for having sexual relations with an underage girl."

"I read about it."

"Maybe you know his ex. She used to be a prosecutor at Cook County. Linda

O'Connell, used to be Linda McDermott. Now she's with some hoity-toity law firm, making the serious money."

"I heard of her. I never had to deal with her."

"She bonded him out yesterday and he boogied."

"Any notion of where he went?"

"No."

"Has he been arrested before?"

Charlie shrugged. "DUIs, maybe a couple of bar complaints, things like that. He's kind of a loser, but he's never gotten involved in anything serious."

"What kind of law does he practice?"

"Mostly what he can get: divorce, workers' compensation, some criminal defense. He tells people he used to be a cop."

"Was he?"

"No." Charlie Mead smiled. "He was a security guard at Loyola when he was in college like, oh, twenty years ago. A campus cop. A wannabe. You know the type. But . . . a hardcore felon? No. That's why it surprises me that he skipped."

"Statutory rape's a serious crime. How old was the girl?"

"Fifteen."

"That's gonna be tough."

"I'm not a lawyer, but I think he could get

probation. Lose his license, but there's no guarantee he would have gone to jail. And now he's jumped." Charlie shrugged again, as if to say it wasn't his problem that the guy had acted guilty and given the District Attorney more ammunition.

"Has he got money?" Maitland said. Meaning, money enough to hide and stay hidden. Money enough to flee to Switzerland or another place uninterested in extraditing a child molester.

"I don't think so," Charlie said. "Like I said, his ex-wife put up the money. He's like a lot of lawyers. Drives a nice car, wears good suits but probably doesn't have more than five thousand he can put hands on."

"Hmmm."

Charlie said, "His pre-trial is set for February second, five days from now. I need him back here by then."

Maitland said, "Thirty thousand?"

"Yeah. Will you do it?"

"Sure."

Charlie placed an eight-by-eleven manila packet on the table, containing the bond application, initial police report, power of attorney and criminal counts.

"Keep me posted," Charlie said.

THREE

Maitland lived alone in a two-bedroom apartment on the northside. He parked his black '94 BMW 750iL in the garage and walked up the back steps to the second floor. On the landing there was a charcoal cooker, chain-locked to the railing, covered with ice that wouldn't melt for two months. In the distance an El-train came and went. Maitland unlocked the door and let himself in.

It was a nice apartment with wood floors and tasteful, modest furnishings. After he and his wife had divorced, he turned the second bedroom into an office where he set up his computer on a table that he had bought for almost nothing because it was supposed to be a Chippendale but wasn't. His wife had been generous, maybe, because she had taken her books and the television and left him most everything else. She had remarried two years ago. Maitland heard from a friend that she recently had a baby and was surprised to find himself feeling a little sad about it.

Maitland cooked chicken in wine sauce

and fettuccini and ate it at the dinner table. Afterwards, he washed the dishes and carried his beer into the living room and turned on CNN. The news bored him, so he switched the channel to a "Friends" re-run and waited for Rachel and Phoebe to get into a squirt gun fight; they didn't, so he turned the television off and put a Dinah Washington CD on and smoked while he read a couple of chapters of the latest Nick Hornby novel.

Before he went to bed, he wrote on a notepad:

1. Call Jackson at DEA. Where did McDermott last use his credit card?
2. Interview Linda O'Connell at her place of work; don't *make appointment.*

FOUR

"Richard, I told you I don' want you smoking in the car."

Maurice (pronounced "Morris") Lee looked over at his younger associate. His expression quiet but firm. Richard didn't look back. He cracked the window, took another draw on the ganja joint to save face, then threw it out. Maurice was meticulous about the car, a dark green '99 Lexus SC400. He drove it steadily down Milwaukee Avenue on their way to see a couple of dem' Crip fellahs who were overdue on payment for guns.

They were Jamaicans.

Maurice wore dark wool slacks and a beige Ralph Lauren cable sweater, black leather gloves and an Armani overcoat. He was thirty, of medium build, with his hair cut close to his scalp. Richard Lawes was younger, twenty-four, and wore a younger man's clothes. A striped sweater that looked like it came from the Gap, jeans and a leather jacket. Richard wore the dreadlocks native to the island, though he had left West Kingston at the age of twelve; brought over by his cousin Maurice, who had joined the Chicago branch of the Raetown Posse years earlier. Men born into a violent world, forged by years of warfare within their own country and a steady diet of imported American gunslinger films, from *The Wild Bunch* to *Rambo III*. They liked movies and could quote every decent Dirty Harry line worth memorizing and some that weren't.

The Lexus turned down an alley, the funnel of the headlights cutting across white and tan garages, then swinging back to the center of the alley. They stopped halfway down the block and pulled in behind a yellowish, hip-hopped ricerocket: Honda Civic with spoilers and Ben-Hur tires, low to the ground. They got out and knocked on the back door of a condominium. A pitbull roared on the other side and between the snarls, a muffled voice yelled out, "Who is it?" in a tone that would have frightened most men back into their vehicles, but Maurice simply said, "Open the door, mon. We got some business to discuss." Irritated, and wanting to get it done.

A black man opened the door. There was another black man standing behind him: short, compact and powerful looking, like the brown and white dog he was holding.

They moved in.

Richard said, "Put that dog away before I shoot him."

The man holding the dog, whose name was Colby, said, "Fuck you."

"Come on, mon," Maurice said. "We are here to talk, that's all."

The man who opened the door was named Kevin. He was big and heavy, bigger than both of the West Indians standing before him. He wore black sweats and gold around his neck. He led them into the kitchen area and said, "What can I do for you?" Playing dumb now. It irritated the Jamaicans, but they kept cool.

Maurice said, "Mon, stop chanting that what-can-I-do-for-you fuckery. We are here to collect the four thousand dollars you owe us and you know it."

There was no wall between the kitchen area and the living room; it was all just one big open space. On the other side of the apartment was a couch facing a big screen television, cable-fed, large colorful images of Matt Damon and John Malkovich playing cards. There were windows near the ceiling and you could see the El tracks outside. There were two bedrooms. Colby put the dog in one of the bedrooms and closed the door. Then he moved into the living room, putting his convict stare onto

Richard. Richard ignored the taunt. The four men found their places and took them: Maurice and Colby on opposite sides of the kitchen counter, Richard behind Maurice a few steps, one eye on the men at the kitchen counter, the other always aware of the short man behind him.

Kevin put his hands on the counter. There was some cheese and bread and a knife there, about eight inches from his hand. Kevin said, "Man, I don't have it. I thought I'd have it this week. But I don't. You know how it is."

Maurice stared at him quietly.

Kevin said, "Man, I don't."

Maurice said, "That is unacceptable."

Kevin cut the coyness, picked up the knife and raised his voice. "I told you motherfucker, I don't have it. Know what I'm saying? It ain't a personal thing here. I ain't dissin' you. I just don't have it."

"We had an agreement."

"Nigger, speak English. Huh? Agreement, toleration . . . you talking to me like I'm fuckin' stupid. You come here with your British nigger lingo bullshit, talking to me like I'm some kind of field hand. Let me tell you something: I don't care how light your skin is, you ain't no better. You hear? Now we can handle this like reasonable men or we can have Colby here do a Mexican tap dance on your ass."

Maurice said, "You asked for guns, we got you guns. Mac-10s, untraceable. We delivered. We had an agreement. You don't pay, and now you threaten us."

"Man, you the one gettin' in my face. Comin' in to *my* house talking to us like we're just a couple a barbershop niggers. I'm a man. You hear me, I'm a man. You show respect. That's all I'm askin'?" Kevin leaned over the kitchen counter now, giving Maurice the convict stare. "Respect."

Maurice kept his voice low, gesturing mildly to Richard. "Oh-kay bredda," Maurice said. And it was the quiet way he said it that threw Kevin, like he meant, "Okay, we'll just leave; come back and discuss it later," but the affirmation had a wholly different meaning. It was a signal, Kevin realized, far too late, as Maurice pulled out a Smith and Wesson 9 millimeter and shot Kevin three times in the chest, the sounds cracking out in the closed room.

Richard's Colt .45 was drawn at the same time Maurice began firing and he turned and put two shots in Colby; the third one missed and thacked in somewhere between Malkovich and Damon, and Colby went down behind the couch. Richard walked past it, stood over Colby and shot him two more times in the head.

Kevin smashed back against the refrigerator, pushing it against the wall, and Maurice leaned over the counter and shot him in the chest a fourth time. Then he took careful aim and shot the dead man in the head.

Outside, they could still hear barking: high-pitched, ferocious and frightened. Getting in the car, Maurice said, "Bloody dog."

"You should have let me shoot the poor thing," Richard said. "It may be days before anyone finds him."

Maurice glanced over at Richard, puzzled, and they drove off.

FIVE

Linda O'Connell was plenty mad.

Maitland said, "I don't think I threatened you."

"Yes you did, you son of a bitch. Yes, you goddam well did. I don't care who you are or what your job is, you don't do that to me. I know what you can and can't do, you understand me. And the next time you do something like this, I'll sue your ass for intentional infliction of emotional distress. I mean that. I do it for a living."

Maitland said, like he was curious, "I thought you worked for a corporate law firm. Don't you usually defend that sort of claim?"

They were sitting at a table in a dark, rather depressing bar with lights advertising Old Style beer, a couple of dirty pool tables and a small television with Star Jones on it. The sound was muted on the television, and the stereo faintly emitted one of Keef and Mick's classics . . . *music on the radio, come on baby, make sweet love to me.* Maitland drank coffee while Linda O'Connell yelled at him, jabbing her cigarette in the air for emphasis. Maitland did not believe he had threatened her, per se, but he had unquestionably blackmailed her. Fifteen minutes earlier he had called the secretary at the law firm at which she worked and said he was a bail enforcement agent searching for Barry McDermott and that he would be up there in fifteen minutes and wouldn't mind sitting in the lobby of Eller and Dietrich for a couple of hours until Ms. O'Connell found the time to meet with him. It would give him a chance to catch up on his reading, he said. Then he said to the secretary, "Do you like to read?" He'd played it up, making his voice gruff and loud and dropping the occasional vulgarity, doing his righteous best to create an image of a bail enforcement agent that looked like he was a roadie for Peter Frampton. He left his cell phone number and Linda O'Connell called him back about three minutes later, saying, "Don't come up here. Do *not* come up here." She didn't have to say that the last thing the senior partners needed to see was her talking with some cracker asshole bounty hunter in the Eller and Dietrich lobby. She didn't have to say it, though she pretty much did.

Maitland had told her they could talk in the Adams Street Bridge bar, which is where he was calling from. It was right

40

down the street from her firm.

"Five minutes," she said and slammed down the phone.

Maitland thought, five minutes she'll give me? Or, she'll be here in five minutes?

She was there in about three minutes, flushed and furious. A fair-skinned woman with red hair that came down to her shoulders. A little on the thin side, worn out and not smiling, but certainly attractive. Maitland stood, made eye contact and said, "Ms. O'Connell?"

She looked back at him, realized that he was the guy and his appearance threw her; she was expecting the big, smelly biker and was instead presented with a rather average-looking man wearing a houndstooth jacket and a blue oxford shirt. But the reprieve was only temporary and the anger and the fear returned in droves and she was on him with the "I don't appreciates" and threats to have his license revoked. It took a while to get her to sit down.

Eventually, Maitland said, "Don't you want your money back?"

"That's not your concern."

"Bringing him back is my concern. I don't, a friend of mine is out three hundred thousand dollars."

"No, he won't. He'll get to keep the

41

money I gave him. He'll only be out two hundred seventy thousand dollars."

"Oh, well, that changes everything."

"I'm sorry about Charlie. But that's the business he's in."

"So he fucked up by trusting you?"

"I'm not the one that fled. Barry did."

"Did you help him?"

"No, I did not."

"You understand that if you did, it's a felony?"

"Better than you know. I was a Cook County ADA for six years. So don't try that cop shit on me."

Maitland leaned back in his chair.

"Okay," he said. "I won't. But let me ask you this: the money aside, do you think it's better for your career if he's brought back or if he gets away?"

Linda O'Connell considered him.

"What do you mean by that?"

"Well, if Barry gets away, if he never stands for trial, people will think that you helped a child molester get away. Fairly or unfairly, that's what they'll think. And I predict this firm will let you go."

"You don't know anything about my profession."

"I know you aren't a criminal defense lawyer. You're a corporate lawyer now, representing banks, insurance companies, that sort of thing. I'll bet the senior partners have already discussed this with you. Am I right?"

"Go to hell."

"But if he's brought back, if it's known that you helped bring him back, the taint will be removed. And you'll be safe."

Linda O'Connell laughed.

"That's a very presumptuous and very simplistic theory," she said. "First of all, I could just as likely be better off if Barry never came back. In a few months, his arrest and the scandal would be forgotten. And my professional life will carry on. Or, it could be argued that no matter what happens, my future at Eller and Dietrich is ruined just because I was associated with Barry. In other words, it probably doesn't mean a snap of the fingers whether I help you or not. So why should I help you?"

Maitland was quiet for a few moments. He studied the woman. She was good-looking, once you got past the seriousness, and she was good at argument. But she was no crook.

Maitland said, "Because you're pissed off at him. He took your money and bolted. He made a fool of you. If you're not angry, then you're insane." He said, "You don't look insane to me."

That got her attention. For a moment Maitland thought she might reach across the table and slap him. But the moment passed and she sighed and leaned back. She took another cigarette from her purse and leaned forward.

"I don't know where he went. I didn't know . . . I didn't know he would run. In fact, I was trying to line him up with this very reputable defense attorney. Alan Baskeyville. He's the one who —"

Maitland said, "I know who he is."

"I had spoken with Alan about the case. He thought that Barry had . . . oh, *fuck!* This just sucks, this whole stupid goddam thing."

Maitland glanced around the bar. Linda was raising her voice now, crying in frustration.

"Thirty thousand dollars . . . goddammit . . . that was most of my savings. And the people I work with are looking at me like I'm some kind of . . . I don't know what. *Idiot,* I suppose. What am I supposed to do?"

Maitland said, "He was your husband."

"Yeah, I suppose. No, that's not right. He was my ex-husband. Or my son; sometimes it's hard to tell the difference."

"Are you still in love with him?"

"You don't know me well enough to ask me that."

"No. But it's a pertinent question."

"How?"

"If you were still in love with him, you'd be more likely to help him run."

"Really," she said flatly. "Have you ever been married, Mr. Maitland?"

"Yes."

"Was she the sort of woman for whom you'd forgive anything?"

"I don't know."

"Maybe you didn't love her then."

Maitland smiled. He didn't want to embarrass the woman, but Jesus . . .

"I think we have different definitions of that sort of thing, Ms. O'Connell."

"Maybe so," she said. "What difference does it make? Barry's gone now."

Oh, shut up, Maitland thought. Bitterness would be preferable to this self-absorbed martyrdom.

Maitland said, "Did he have a girl?"

"He had lots of girls."

"Who was he seeing lately?"

"I don't know. Sometimes a girl answered the phone at his house. She may still be there."

"What's her name?"

"I don't know her real name," Linda said.

"Her stage name was Cinnamon Barefoot."

And Maitland thought, stage name? It sounded like that of a professional dancer. The sort that takes her clothes off in front of crowds of men.

It turned out that she was.

SIX

Maitland drove to a Starbucks, ordered an espresso, sat down and called Jay Jackson, an old friend of his from DEA.

Jay said, "How's the furniture business?"

"Not too good. I still have to do some bounty hunting, make ends meet."

"Yeah, tell me anything, I'm black." Jay said, "You only take the big ones; you can afford to turn down the small ones. Am I right or am I right?"

"You're right, baby. Rich as Midas." Maitland said, "You read about Barry McDermott? He's a lawyer that was accused of statutory rape. He jumped bail. No one seems to know where he is."

"Yeah, I read about it. She comes from money, that girl."

"Who?"

"The fifteen-year-old girl. Her daddy owns some sort of cancer clinic."

Maitland said, "How did you know that?"

"It was in the *Reader*. You didn't see it?"

"No. Not in the *Reader*."

"Yeah, they showed her picture. She don't look too innocent herself. Newspaper suggested she was pretty wild."

"She's fifteen. Consent isn't an issue."

"I know that, man. I got a daughter that age. I'm just saying I can see how it happens, that's all."

"Jay, it's too early in the morning to have this conversation. I need a favor from you."

"Yeah?"

"Can you hook into the NCIS there and tell me where Barry McDermott last used his credit card? In particular, I need you to look for . . . strip joints, gentlemen's clubs. He was seeing a dancer named Cinnamon Barefoot. Also, I need to get some indication of where he's run to. So you should look to see where he's used it the past two days."

"All right. Give me fifteen minutes."

Maitland sipped his espresso and read the *Sun-Times*. Roger Ebert panned the new Jennifer Lopez romantic comedy, saying she was actually a pretty good actress and didn't understand this desperate, Meg Ryan-like need to show audiences she was a sweetheart. Mark Steyn wrote about Bill Clinton and asked if it was possible to impeach an ex-president. Maureen Dowd wrote a column making some sort of strained analogy between Donald Rumsfeld and one of Carrie's boyfriends from "Sex and the City" and Maitland gave up about halfway through.

Then his cell phone rang and it was Jackson.

"Ohhh-kay then. He got gasoline apparently at a convenience store in Merchant, Kansas. That's about forty miles south of Kansas City. That was yesterday. That's the last time he used his American Express card. As to the gentlemen's clubs, he seems to favor a joint called the Admiral."

Maitland said, "Merchant, Kansas. That's it?"

"Yeah. How much is the bounty?"

"Movie money, man. Just movie money," Maitland said. "Thanks, Jay. Have your wife call me sometime; I'll give her a deal on an antique table."

"Movie money my ass. Hey, you bring this guy back," Jay said, "you *give* her the table."

"Later," Maitland smiled and hung up.

The Admiral was like a lot of strip joints: dark blue and black, cold and smelling like a smoke-filled igloo. It was before noon and the place wouldn't open for table dances for a few hours. Maitland had rung the bell, shown his BEA badge and bluffed the manager into letting him in. It was after that that the manager realized that

49

Maitland wasn't a cop. He didn't seem to get sore about it.

"Cinnamon? She got greedy with the stage time and shoved one of the other girls so I gave her a couple of weeks off to let her think about what she'd done. I haven't seen her since then."

Maitland showed the manager McDermott's picture.

"This is the guy I'm looking for. Did you ever see him?"

"Yeah, I've seen him. He was a pretty steady customer."

Maitland said, "I understand she moved in with him."

The manager was in his late forties, graying black hair and a stomach straining against a blue denim shirt. He held his hands up. "That's her business."

Maitland said, "The guy's name is Barry McDermott. Do you remember that name?"

"No. What'd he do?"

"He is alleged to have had sexual relations with an underage girl."

"How underage?" The manager seemed worried now, like maybe it had been one of his performers.

"Fifteen."

"The youngest girl we got here is nineteen. I swear."

"I'm not asking about that," Maitland said. "Okay?"

"This is a clean business."

"Right. Listen, do you know if the girl moved in with McDermott or not?"

"She may have. Really, I don't know. Look, when she was here, she had a day job too. Waited tables at a bar and grill called . . . the Maproom. It's in Bucktown. You might find her there."

"Okay. You got a picture of her I can take with me?"

He led Maitland to his office computer where he had a webpage of colorful stills of the girls: young, shiny, hard looking otters with names like Kendra, Jennipher, Ranna and Tarra. There were pictures of them together and pictures of them apart. Each had her own page with an individual biography. There was a picture of Cinnamon Barefoot where she was on all fours, wearing a tight bikini, knees and hands submerged in a pool of water that was supposed to reflect but didn't. The photograph was the work of an amateur. Cinnamon looked up into the camera with an expression of such strained seductiveness it would drive Roger Vadim to shake his head in pathos.

Her bio said:

51

Hey, my name is Cinnamon. I am 23 years old and I am from Skokie.
I enjoy water skiing, drag racing, working out and traveling.
I am currently pursuing a career in the medical field.
I love being an Admiral's dancer and look forward to meeting you.

"You can take that one if you like," the manager said. "Though I have to warn you, they look different off stage."

He was right about that. She was one of two waitresses on duty for the lunch hour on a post-Superbowl Saturday and was easy to pick out. One of the waitresses was a red-haired girl with apple cheeks and a ruddy complexion and she looked like she taught Wednesday night CCD to eighth graders and enjoyed it. The other had heavily permed hair that was some kind of blonde and hoop earrings. A body that could pass for fat in modern fashion, but that was full and ripe and inviting off the modeling ramps of Paris. Large-breasted and earthy if you like them that way, which Maitland did. But then he liked them a lot of ways.

But she was off-stage and out of make-up and you could see the tired look in her eyes.

When he was a policeman, Maitland had worked vice for a year before going undercover full-time. He had met plenty of the bad girls. He liked women, but what struck him about the prostitutes and the strippers and the party girls was their remarkable sameness. The drugs, the booze and the self-delusion. The continuing belief that they were meant for better things, like a shot on "Survivor" or a gig as a Bud-Lite girl. Maybe this one would be different.

He seated himself at her station and waited for her to take his order. He gave her a nice smile when she brought the first beer, but got no response. When she brought him the house spaghetti and meatballs, he said, "You know, I think I've seen you before."

The woman said, "Yeah?" Tentative and unenthusiastic.

"Yeah. You're a dancer, aren't you?"

"Sometimes. What are you?"

"I'm a lawyer."

"Yeah?"

"Yeah. Personal injury."

"Ambulance chaser, huh?" She seemed to be interested now, just.

"There's a lot of money in ambulances. You used to work at the Admiral?"

"I quit that shithole. They don't appreciate real talent."

"Ah, I knew it. You quit, huh? You going out to Hollywood or something?"

"I've thought about it. I don't know. You know Hollywood?"

"You know what? A buddy of mine from high school, Fritz Haas, he went out there about ten years ago with about three hundred dollars in his pocket. No job lined up out there, no prospects at all. He just wanted to write for the movies. He got a job at a hotel in Beverly Hills working room service. He was so poor, he got by by eating people's leftovers. Ten months later, he sells a screenplay to a studio. I forgot what the movie was about — something about a bunch of college students going snow-skiing and one by one they all start getting killed. I don't remember the name of it, but it had that girl that used to be on that witch show in it."

"Rose McGowan?"

Maitland regarded her interest.

"She the one with the brown hair?"

"Yeah, that's her," she said. "That's her."

"Yeah, it was her. Anyway, the movie ends up making all this money in video sales and then the studio commissions Fritz to write three more. Eventually, he starts producing his own stuff and he's richer than anyone I've ever known. Now some network is paying him all this money to develop his own television show." Maitland said, "I'm sorry, I suppose all this movie talk is boring you."

"No, it's interesting. What's the show about?"

"It's about, uh. . . ."

"You jerk," she said. "There is no television show, is there?"

Maitland looked at her deadpan, then burst into laughter. "No. I'm sorry. It's just that you're so beautiful. You just drive a man to make shit up."

The girl smiled and shook her head.

"What's your name, cowboy?"

"Evan."

"Evan, you should learn a different approach." She said, "You got money?"

"Sure."

"Party money?" She had her hand on his thigh now, under the table.

"Sure." Maitland said, "Hey, how do you know I'm not a cop?"

"Are you?"

"No."

"Uh-huh. Well a cop wouldn't have laid that Fritz Hart crap on me."

"Fritz Haas."

Cinnamon Barefoot moved her hand up Maitland's leg and cupped his genitals. She put her mouth close to his face.

With lowered voice that was almost husky, she said, "Five hundred dollars, Fritz Haas."

"My oh my," Maitland said. "When do we get off?"

SEVEN

The townhouse was near the bar, in a neighborhood that had once been the home of aging hippies and artists and other failed bohemians before the unseen hand of market forces had pushed them out and replaced them with lawyers and MBAs and Range Rovers and well-kept dog parks.

Cinnamon Barefoot led Maitland up the steps and inside. He watched her bottom swinging to and fro and thought briefly of the Nair commercial with the girls singing, *"Who wears short shorts? Da-da-da-da-dada-da da. We wear short shorts."*

The place was tastefully decorated, with oak floors and plantation shutters on the windows and Danish furniture. But it was dirty. There were dishes piled up in the sink and newspapers strewn about the floor, like the owner had had an argument with his housecleaner.

Maitland asked for directions to the bathroom.

She told him and then walked up the stairs.

In the bathroom, he found a copy of

Maxim magazine next to the toilet and the address label said Barry McDermott. He had already recognized the street and house number from the bond application, but he felt better when he saw the man's name on the magazine. You will be found, Mr. McDermott. You will be found.

Maitland walked out of the bathroom to see Cinnamon standing on the stairway wearing a white cotton T-shirt and under-pants. The shirt and the panties were thin and rather sheer if one cared to look. He looked up at her and she looked down at him. She spread her hands in one of those disgracefully arousing how-do-you-like-the-goodies? gestures and Maitland found himself wondering how much he really valued $500.00.

But what he said was, "I just saw some dude's name on a magazine. Are you living here with a boyfriend?"

"Don't worry about it," she said. "He's not here."

"So you are living with someone."

"He's out of town."

"Where did he go?"

"Fuck, I don't know. Relax, will you."

"I just don't want any trouble."

"He's out of town and he's not coming back for a long time. Okay?"

"How do you know that?"

"Jesus, Evan, stop being such a woman. I just know. I don't get my kicks watching two guys fight over me, all right." She said, "Now are you coming upstairs or not?"

He went up to her. They kissed in the middle of the staircase and, prostitute or no, the kiss was good. Maitland placed his hands on her thighs and slid them up to tug down her panties, in danger of creating some sort of *Risky Business* moment then and there, but she pushed him off and began walking up the stairs.

"Honey, I may earn it on my back, but there's a limit."

They reached the second floor. It was a small hallway between two rooms. Cinnamon stripped off her shirt and walked into the bedroom. Maitland stood in the hall, on the brink, but then turned and looked into the other room. There was a desk and a computer in there.

Maitland walked into the other room.

"Hey," Cinnamon said. "Where are you going?"

"Just a minute, baby."

He sat down at the desk and looked at the computer screen. It told him he had mail and that was too good to pass up. He moved the mouse to the icon and clicked it open.

The message read:

Hey asshole! Where the hell are you? The police are looking for you and they are going to find you. You don't have any money and you've got no place to go. Please don't do this. Call me. It's the best thing. I know we can get this thing straightened out. Please call. Please.

Linda

Well, he thought, it looks like Linda O'Connell was telling the truth. Which was good for her, but not much help to Maitland here and now. He clicked onto the "old mail" bar and pulled up the last few days worth of e-mail. There were a few more from Linda, others from names that were not easily identifiable. He saw the e-mail name DKittyKat at aol.com.

That got his attention.

There are runners who plan ahead. They have secret hideouts and offshore bank accounts and contacts in countries that won't extradite American fugitives. But those sort are rare. Then there are the runners that can live in the wild and survive off the land, sometimes indefinitely. Latter-day mountain men who can disappear into the Appalachians and never be found. They're even more rare.

The majority of runners are not that resourceful. They're normal, they're human. And being human, they seek shelter in and with those things that are entirely predictable, i.e., food and/or pussy. Families will provide them with food, but family members are easily discovered. Women are something else.

It was a reasonably safe bet that DKittyKat was of the female persuasion. And Linda O'Connell's foolish loyalty to Barry McDermott was evidence that he could be something of a charmer where the ladies were concerned. Perhaps he was hiding out with this kittycat.

Maitland pulled up an e-mail from DKittyKat that had been sent ten days earlier. It said:

You're the one that's naughty. If you remember, it was your idea to rent those movies. Am dying of boredom down here . . . miss Chicago!!!! Miss you too. . . .

Well, well, Maitland thought. Naughty talk. And she lives out of town.

"What are you doing?"

Cinnamon stood behind him, just inside the room. Still naked from the waist up, but not striking any poses now. She had busted him and was looking more than a little irritated.

Maitland met her accusatory stare, held it, as he walked toward her. He placed his hands firmly on her waist then pushed her out the door, shut and locked it.

"Hey!"

Bam bam!

"Hey! Hey! Open this goddam door! What are you doing in there? Huh? You fucking freak, what are you doing?"

She went on like that, shouting and pounding and calling him names, while Maitland printed out every DKittyKat e-mail he could find. He folded the hard copies and put them in his jacket pocket. Then he opened the door, quickly and making something of a show of it.

It worked. Cinnamon shrunk back from him.

"Who are you?" she said.

"Never mind that," Maitland said. "Who is DKittyKat? A friend of yours? Another dancer?"

"What?"

"Answer me, dammit. Who is she?"

"I don't know, okay? I don't know."

"This ain't a game, lady. Your daddy is in big trouble. Now if you lie to me, I can make your life very unpleasant. Do you understand that?"

"This is my home."

"Yes, and you invited me in. And, I might add, offered to fuck me for money." Maitland said, "Are you getting the picture now?"

"You are a cop, aren't you. I knew it."

"Just tell me where he went. That's all I want."

"I don't know where he went." She said, "I don't."

Maitland picked up her shirt and tossed it to her. He was getting distracted. Cinnamon held it against her chest.

"Hey," she said. "If I knew I would tell you. I mean, look around. Do you think I give a shit about him?"

Good point, Maitland thought. Besides, she seemed genuinely frightened of him and some gross, ex-cop part of him took pleasure in it.

"Okay," he said. He handed her a fifty. "For your trouble," he said.

He walked down the stairs to let himself out.

From his car, he made a call.
"Tim?"
"Yeah."

"It's Evan Maitland."

"Hey, Evan."

"Listen, can I come by? I've got an e-mail address. And I need to match it to a name and address."

"Sure," Tim said. "We'll be here."

Tim Bernard lived in a loft with three roommates. He was about thirty, though he could pass for twenty-four. When Maitland got to his place, Tim was still in his bathrobe. There was a girl of about twenty sitting on the couch watching a big screen television. Tim said, "That's Claudine." She wore jeans and a T-shirt that said, "On a rebound, you'll do." Claudine waved to Maitland and Maitland waved back.

Maitland gave Tim the paper with the e-mail address. Tim shuffled off to his computer.

Tim said, "Make yourself at home. You want a beer, there's one in the fridge."

"No thanks."

A guy came down the stairs, recognized Maitland and said hello.

"Hey, Evan. What you got going on?"

"Hey, Mark. Just work."

Mark was Tim's partner in their business. Though their business was hard to define. They used to have some sort of dot-com enterprise and they made enough money off that to retire, smart enough to get out before the bubble burst. They were affable guys, younger than Maitland and had been effectively able to retire before Maitland could. But Maitland managed not to envy them. Their retirement seemed to amount to a lot of cable television and assorted roommates. But they were nice guys. They had good taste in furniture and they knew the Internet.

Mark said, "You still got the 750?"

Mark was into cars.

"Yeah," Maitland said.

Mark said, "Just bought the new 635 with the six-speed. Oh, it's sweet. It's a rocket."

Maitland estimated the price tag at around seventy grand. Mark had probably paid cash. Mark was twenty-nine years old.

"Really?" Maitland said.

"Yeah. It's out in the garage. You want to take it for a drive?"

"Ah, I can't now, Mark. Work."

"I hear you, man."

Maitland looked over at Tim sitting at the computer. He was still working on it.

Maitland gestured to the girl on the couch. "New roommate?" he said.

"Yeah, she's with Tim." Mark lowered his voice. "Pretty hot, huh?"

"Yeah, she's pretty."

"Tim. I don't know how he does it. I mean, look at him. Sits around in his bathrobe, probably hasn't had a bath in days, smokes cigarettes like a chimney. People think it's because he's got money. But I knew him when he had nothing and it was the same then."

Maitland said, "He's a confident man."

Tim said, "Okay, Evan, I think I got something."

Maitland drifted over to the computer.

Tim said, "I can't find a present address for this woman. But I can tell you where this account was created. It was at a law firm, here in Chicago. See, here's the list of names at that address. There's three of them."

Maitland said, "So it's one of these three people."

"Well," Tim said, "it's probably not this guy. Then you've got two people left. Women. There is Ellen Tracy and Diane Creasey. 'D' is probably Diane Creasey."

Tim printed out a sheet and handed it to Maitland.

EIGHT

The long dark cloud is comin' down
Feel I'm knockin' on heaven's door
Knock, knock, knockin' on heaven's
*   door*
Knock, knock, knockin' on heaven's
*   door . . .*

Trevor Jim leaned back in his chair and let the Dylan seep in. To him, it was a lovely, soulful tune. Quiet and sad and romantic, capturing the gunfighter's plight. He kills and kills again, but he gets tired and he gets frightened. He's only a man, after all. Trevor Jim had killed many men, in Jamaica and in the States. He had started out as an enforcer for the Jamaican Labor Party (JLP) at the age of sixteen and moved his way up. Like many Jamaican youths, he had not imagined he would live past the age of twenty and was surprised when he did. He felt the sort of luck a man feels when he lives past his mark. It almost made him feel that he was indestructible, immortal. It made him dangerous.

Trevor Jim said, "Barry's not a gangster. He is a lawyer. You know how they are."

Maurice said, "Is that why you trusted him?"

"Oh, don't accuse me of that, Maurice; we known each other too long. I did not trust him. I simply did not imagine that he would do this. We cyan predict everything."

"Did you know he was involved with the girl?"

Trevor said, "No, I did not know about the girl. It was bad timing."

His full name was Trevor Collins. Like the men who worked for him, he also was heavily influenced by the gunslinger lore. Not the sort of influence gained by reading Zane Grey novels or an actual visit to the dry, barren climates of Wyoming or Colorado. Rather, the lore as taught by the movies. But Trevor was older, forty now, and he had seen *The Dirty Dozen* over a dozen times. In the moviehouses of Montego Bay, he had swelled with pride when Jim Brown told Lee Marvin (the coolest white man ever to be in the movies, cooler even than Pacino), "That's your war, major. Not mine." Had cheered when Jim Brown sprinted away from the chalet, throwing grenades down the chutes onto the trapped Nazis. Had wept when the Germans cut him down with machine guns.

Who in Jamaica *didn't* want to be Jim

Brown? Trevor was tall and big and athletic and kept his hair cut close to the scalp. But apart from that and being black, his resemblance to Jim Brown was negligible. And then, glory be, he had been in a gunfight in a Kingston dance hall. He killed six members of a rival gang, more than any of his mates, and afterwards someone said of him, "You *cyan* kill this one. He a regular Jim Brown." The ultimate compliment. But there was already a Jim Brown then, a Jamaican Jim Brown who was also legend, even though he was dead. So the name became Trevor Jim. Which was all right with him.

He sat with Maurice in his Lakeshore condominium, pondering what to do about the lawyer that had turned thief and run off with $800,000 of their money.

Maurice said, "Perhaps it is not such a bad thing. Had he not jumped bail, he may have offered to give us up to the police. A trade."

Trevor Jim nodded. "I had thought of that myself. But he not a Rambo type'a fellah, can go into the woods and stay hidden; he not a crook. He's hiding somewhere, but he don't know what to do. So they going to catch him and then he probably want to use my money to hire a good lawyer."

Maurice said, "I don't know where he is."

"Find him," Trevor Jim said. "Bring my money back here."

"And Barry? Shall we make an example of him?"

Trevor Jim knew all about making examples. The posse signature four shots to the body, one to the head. The use of knives and hatchets and other voodoo insignia which Western civilization snorted at as primitive, but which was taken very seriously by West Indians and the federal task forces familiar with their gangs. The terrifying marks they use to send messages to people that cross them.

But, Trevor Jim thought, for Barry McDermott? He had stolen $800,000.00 in heroin money from them, but he was hardly a man. He was certainly no warrior. It didn't seem fitting to make an example of him.

"It isn't necessary," Trevor Jim said. "He is a civilian. Just kill him and bring the money back."

NINE

Attorney Tony Burns said, "Did you read about the suit against the City of Chicago involving the city's street maintenance workers?"

Maitland said, "No, I didn't."

"The street workers, they clean the city's streets, move garbage, clear fallen trees, that sort of thing. They work in the cold and the rain and they receive very little pay for it. And their union is weak. They're poor men; most of them are black."

Tony Burns was a tall, thin man in his mid-fifties. He had an aristocrat's jaw and he took his time when he spoke. The office was not a sharp one, but rather homey. There was a lamp on the desk that looked like it might have come from a Wisconsin cabin, and there was a golden retriever sleeping on the rug in the corner. Tony Burns had gestured to the dog after he let Maitland in his office, saying, "This is Roger." Like he was an associate.

Now, Maitland saw the drift of Tony Burns' conversation, somewhat, and decided he'd let the guy continue with it.

Maitland said, "Okay."

"One of the facilities they operate out of is called Ridgewood. It's walled in to prevent people from stealing or vandalizing the city's snowplows and equipment. The men park their personal vehicles inside those walls in the morning and then drive them out at the end of their shift. One day, a chainsaw disappeared. So the supervisors closed the gates of the Ridgewood facility and locked thirty of their employees in and forced them to open up the trunks of their vehicles and submit to a search. They kept them there until every vehicle was searched. They never found the chainsaw, of course. But they violated all those men's Fourth Amendment rights and subjected them to false imprisonment."

Maitland said, "And then these gentlemen hired you, correct?"

"They did," Tony Burns said. "I sued the City. They did not offer to settle, so I took them to court and got a jury to award those men twenty thousand dollars apiece."

"That's very commendable," Maitland said. "And I think I know why you told me about it."

"Do you."

Maitland ignored the man's dry imperiousness. Perhaps he'd earned it.

72

"Yes," Maitland said. "You want to make it clear to me that you're not afraid to take on authority. And that you understand the law better than I do. Is that pretty much where you're going with it?"

Tony Burns nodded. "More or less. Barry McDermott and I are not close friends. In fact, I wouldn't even say we're friends. But we have shared office space for many years. And it's important that you know that I won't be bullied into helping you put him in prison."

"I think you misunderstand me, Mr. Burns. I'm not a police officer. I am a bail enforcement agent. A mere citizen, like you. Or those street cleaners. It's not within my power to deny him due process."

Tony Burns smiled.

"Oh, Mr. Maitland, you are clever. Reducing yourself to the rank of a street cleaner to gain my sympathy. Did you used to be a policeman?"

"Yes."

"I thought so." He said it without patronizing him. "I am familiar with the Supreme Court's ruling on bounty hunters. As a profession, you are not known for being especially mindful of civil rights. Given that, why should a libertarian like myself offer you assistance?"

"Because I'm not a policeman. I'm just a courier. I'm going to bring him back and then he'll be judged by a jury." He said, "Besides, I don't get the feeling you like Barry very much."

"Whether or not I like him is beside the point. He has rights."

"Uh-huh," Maitland said. "Diane Creasey was your legal assistant, yes?"

"Yes," Burns said, momentarily taken aback. "Who told you that?"

"Everybody in this office knows about it," Maitland said.

"Okay, she was. So what?"

"I have reason to think that Diane Creasey is harboring him."

"What?"

"I said I have reason to think Diane Creasey is harboring him. When she worked here, did they have an affair?"

"I don't know —"

"I think you do know."

Tony Burns' face flushed, and for a moment he almost broke his controlled expression. Maitland felt embarrassed for him. Because two things now seemed moderately clear. One, Diane Creasey *had* been having an affair with Barry McDermott. Two, that if the existence of that affair had not broken accomplished trial lawyer Tony

Burns' heart, it had at least taken a good whack at his primal ego. Men will be men.

"Yes," Burns said. "They were having an affair."

Maitland almost said he was sorry, but thought better of it. The lawyer seemed like an all-right guy and there was no need to humiliate him.

Tony Burns said, "Why do you think she's harboring him?"

"I did a cross-check on an e-mail address and it matched up with someone named Diane Creasey. Then I found out that she worked here."

Tony Burns looked bewildered.

"So why did you have to talk to me?"

"I needed to confirm that they had been lovers."

"Oh."

A couple of awkward moments passed. Maitland held in his condolences and said, "Where did she go?"

"She quit working here a year and a half ago. She married a soldier and left town with him."

"What was the soldier's name?"

The man seemed to stare off into space. Then he said, "Johnson. Jeff Johnson. He was a fucking idiot."

Geez, Maitland thought, another lawyer

in love. Still bitter over a woman who probably wasn't worth his time, preferring bad boy Barry McDermott to him. In some faultless, human way, the same passion that moved him to defend a bunch of impoverished street cleaners led him to fall for a legal assistant that didn't give a flip about him. It would be nice to pick and choose the people you care for, but most of us don't have that luxury.

Maitland said, "Where was he posted?"

"Oklahoma," Burns said. "An Air Force base in Oklahoma."

Maitland went back to his apartment and did a skip trace on Jeff Johnson on his computer. He was stationed at Tinker Air Force Base in Midwest City, Oklahoma, a suburb of Oklahoma City. He called the base and learned that Sergeant Johnson had shipped out to Turkey three months earlier, providing air support for the war in Iraq.

That's all the sign I need, Maitland thought.

He packed a bag for three days' worth of travel. If he couldn't find McDermott in that amount of time, he'd be wasting his time and his money. Too much time away from the store, literally.

He stored his luggage in the trunk of his

750iL along with his Glock .45, two sets of handcuffs and a belly chain in case the skipper proved to be difficult. He stored a Smith and Wesson .38 snub nose in the glove compartment.

He called Bianca from I-55 after he'd gotten outside the city, free of the endless stop signs and traffic lights. It was cold and overcast as the Chicago skyline became distant in the rearview mirror.

Bianca said, "When were you planning on telling me you were leaving?"

"We're partners, Bianca. Not manager and assistant."

She was quiet for a moment, and Maitland could tell she was irritated. She said, "Okla-homa, uh? Like a cowboy."

"It's just a city. Like Chicago, but smaller."

"Yeah," she said. "How long you be gone?"

"About three days. Maybe four. How's business today?"

"I made a couple of sales. But it's starting to snow, now. I'm not expecting many more customers."

Maitland looked at the gray highway before him. He didn't see any snow, but he could see it coming.

Bianca said, "We're supposed to get some

chairs from New Hampshire Friday. I'm a gonna need you here then."

"I'll be back by then."

She gave a disappointing grunt. Like, yeah, maybe.

Maitland said, "Stop sounding like a wife."

"I am a wife," she said.

"Not mine," Maitland said.

He heard her smile through the phone. "Okay, Evan. You be careful, uh."

"I will. I'll see you."

Maitland clicked the cell phone off and set it on the console. Light flakes began drifting onto the windshield and he turned the wipers on.

TEN

As Evan Maitland checked into a depressing motel room forty miles from Branson, Missouri, Detective Julie Ciskowski interviewed a witness named Sherita Horn.

Sherita was a black female of twenty years, who had called the police from an apartment on South Milwaukee Avenue and reported that two of her friends were dead.

She was hysterical: crying and frightened. Young, broke and pregnant.

Julie Ciskowski thought she was lying.

Detective Ciskowski said, "You heard the shots, right?"

"Yeah," Sherita said. "I heard the shots. I just didn't see nothing, you know."

"Why is it you didn't see anything?"

"Because I was hiding. In the bedroom? Kevin and Colby was out there in the living room, talking to some guys. And then they started shooting. So I just stayed in there with the dog? Then I called the police."

"You said guys," Julie said. "There was more than one?"

"That's what I think. I don't really know,

though. I didn't hear nothing."

"Did you hear what they were saying?"

"No I didn't."

The girl was tall and thin, taller than Julie Ciskowski. But she was young and unsure of herself. She felt intimidated by the lady cop, standing there in her tan trench coat draped over blue jeans and a red sweater, a Glock .40 on her hip. Looking fashionable and cute, with her fair skin and curly dark hair, but hard and suspicious-like. A police lady.

They were standing outside the apartment amidst a couple of patrol cars and other police vehicles. It was cold and unwelcome, but Sherita did not want to go back in there and smell the blood and the death.

Julie Ciskowski said, "Sherita?"

"Yeah."

"You heard them talk, right?"

"I heard — you know. I heard voices."

"Who was Kevin expecting?"

"I don't know."

"Okay. Why did you wait almost a whole day to call the police?"

"I — you know — I don't know. I had . . . stuff."

"You had stuff. To take care of?"

Sherita Horn looked right, telling the experienced detective she was thinking of a lie.

Julie said, "Are you scared?"

"Yeah," Sherita said. "I'm scared."

"Gangsters?"

"I don't know."

"Sherita, look at me. If it was gangsters, you're better off telling me about it than not telling me about it. You know that?"

"No. I don't know that."

"If you're not telling me something you know, then you're obstructing the investigation. And you can get in trouble for that. You don't want that, do you?"

"No. I don't want that. I don't want to die neither."

Julie sighed. "Were they black voices or white voices?"

Sherita looked away.

Julie said, "You can tell me that."

"Black voices."

"Anyone you know?"

"No," she said firmly. "No one I know."

"So you didn't recognize their voices."

"They was . . . they was Island voices? Know what I'm saying?"

"*Island* voices? You mean, like foreign?"

"Yeah."

"Like how did they sound?"

"Yah, mon. Like that."

"Jamaicans?"

"Man, I don't know."

"They were Jamaican, then."

"I think so."

"What were they arguing about?"

After a moment, Sherita said, "Guns. Money. Okay? Like, you happy now?"

Julie Ciskowski put it down on her notepad.

"Did Kevin buy guns from these guys?"

"Yeah, probably. But I don't know nothing about that."

"You just said you did."

"I just said, probably. That's what I said."

Detective John Galvan returned from the counter with two old-style hot dogs piled with white onions and green peppers and an order of fries. He took a seat across from Julie. Julie wasn't hungry, but she put out her cigarette so her partner could eat.

Galvan said, "So you think it's Jamaican posse?"

"Oh, yeah," Julie said. "A dispute over guns, payment for guns. Four shots to the body, one to the head."

"They're very vengeful."

"And reckless. They'd just as well leave a brand on the victim's chest."

"But which posse?"

"That shouldn't be hard to figure out. We round up some people in Kevin's gang and find out who supplied them with their Mac-10s."

"I can talk with Ed Ryan at the task force tomorrow. He can probably help us."

Julie Ciskowski looked out the window onto the cold, dark street and the traffic passing by.

"It doesn't change, does it?"

Galvan said, "What do you mean?"

"Eighty years ago, it was Capone shooting up the city. Fifteen years ago, it was Crips and Bloods. Now it's Posses. Gang wars. It changes form, but the thing itself doesn't go away."

"Human nature," Galvan said. "We do what we can."

But Julie continued to stare out the window.

John Galvan was a big man, six foot four and weighing in at two-sixty, not much of it fat. A macho fellow that, if wearing a Laura Ashley dress and a sun hat, would still look like a plainclothes cop. But like many detectives, he had a moderate amount of compassion and generosity. Like every other cop in the city, he was aware that six months earlier little Julie Ciskowski had shot and killed a man on the Lafayette Station El platform. A crazy man that had walked up the stairs and stood in front of the train firing off rounds from an AK-47. He had killed two people and wounded another by the time the first set of patrol officers showed up. Detectives Galvan and Ciskowski happened to get there soon after it started, having heard the shots-fired call on the police radio. They were calling in the tactical team, but it was taking too long. Standing among the big uniformed cops like so many trees, five foot five Julie Ciskowski had said, "We don't have time to wait" and before anyone could say much else she called over a woman nearby and borrowed her frumpy looking hat and her ugly over-coat. She put it on and suddenly gained the appearance of a meek little librarian. Walked up the stairs by herself and slipped into the crowd of terrified commuters being held at bay by the rifle-bearing madman. She merged her way to the front of the quiv-ering mass, but stayed off to the side, out of the madman's periphery, got to the fringe and then saw the person behind the terror, pointing the rifle at the crowd then up in the air. She heard him shout something about democracy being a joke before taking her Glock .40 out of her coat pocket and shooting him three times in the chest and body.

John Galvan thought the lady cop had

been low ever since because she didn't have the soul of a killer. That she was torn up with regret and remorse and shame for having killed a man that needed to be killed.

He was wrong. Julie Ciskowski *was* sad. But not because she had killed the madman. She was sad because her marriage was falling apart and had been ever since the shooting.

It was after the shooting that her husband had started mistreating her. Not physically; Dan Ciskowski knew better than to do that. And her husband was not a physical man. A classic passive-aggressive, he was a corrector. He corrected her grammar, her eating habits, her knowledge of current affairs, her conversation at parties, even her conduct in the bedroom — though this was becoming less and less of a concern these days. He was driving her crazy. She sometimes wondered if she should shoot *him*.

It was all the more painful because they had once been such a great couple. The kind that meets in college and finds out they love the same books and movies and music and have similar views about God and Ronald Reagan. That persuade themselves that there is such a thing as soul mates and them soul mates is us. He had made her laugh then. It was difficult to believe that it was only a few years ago he had made her laugh. After college, he had started a computer company and had been quite successful at it. She had worked for a year and a half at a financial services company, had almost died of boredom, before taking the police academy entrance examination. The department recruiters had told her that if she became a police officer, the city would pay for her law school. And, at that time, Dan had said it sounded like a wonderful opportunity. So she signed up, graduated near the top of her class at the academy and was sworn in at the age of twenty-six. Seven years had since passed. She never did go to law school. But she did become a respected detective. And then, six months ago, a hero. The little lady cop that took out the Lafayette Station madman.

And her life had been pretty crappy ever since.

She looked across the table at John. For a moment, she considered unloading on him. She liked him, after all. He was respectful toward her and, even before the shooting, had never patronized her or come on to her. He was married and, thankfully, kept his private life to himself. John was a religious man. He attended Catholic mass every Sunday and observed all the holy days. It was a part of his life. At times, Julie envied his faith. She wanted to say to him now, partner to partner, human to human, "I don't want to become another divorced cop."

But she didn't. John was all right. But she feared that if she opened up to him, even with the best intentions, he might later let it slip in the locker room that his partner was going through a rough time with her husband. And then a pack of hyena cops would come sniffing around, thinking that she was open for business. Jesus. Horny cops. That was all she needed.

"We do what we can," he said.

"Yeah," Julie said. She took one of his fries and bit into it. "That's all we can do."

ELEVEN

They finished making love and Diane got out of bed and went to the bathroom. She came back with a white towel, rubbed it between her thighs and threw it on the floor. Then she lit a cigarette. The smoke wafted up and pushed its way into the rank smell of cats and Barry thought he would die. Diane had three cats, one of which never left her bedroom. Barry watched her movement with the towel, wondering why she couldn't have done that in the bathroom. He had been staying with her now for two days and the cats and the smoke and the hand lotion were starting to get to him. The sex was still good, though. The sex had always been good with Diane.

Barry had not told her there was a warrant for his arrest. He felt he could; Diane had never been the judgmental type. One of her boyfriends had once stabbed a guy over a parking space and she had done little more than shrug at it. She had stayed with that boyfriend until he left her for someone else. So she was not the gasping type.

Still, Barry had not told he was on the

run. He saw no reason to complicate things at this stage. Besides, if he told her he had been arrested for statutory rape, she wouldn't so much ask, "Did you do it?" as she would, "What are you going to do?" And he didn't have an answer for that. He hadn't figured it out yet.

Lying beside him, Diane said, "Do you want to watch TV?"

"I don't know," Barry said. "What time is it?"

"About ten o'clock."

"What's on?"

"There was this special on John Wayne Macy I wanted to watch. A&E, I think."

"Macy. You mean, Gacy, right?"

"Was that his name?"

"Yeah."

"Oh."

He waited for her to ask what he wanted to do.

But she said, "Well, I'm going to go watch it."

Inconsiderate bitch.

"Yeah, okay."

She put a shortie bathrobe on and walked down the hall. A minute later he heard the muffled roar of the television. She was a petite woman with short frosted hair. Barry, who had made love to her at least fifty times, thought she had a good figure but wasn't very pretty in the face. She had once said to him that people thought she looked like Cameron Diaz and did he think so too? Barry gave her the lawyer's bogus look of contemplation and then said, "You know, you do, kind of." A close fucking call.

The first night, she would have asked him what he wanted to do. She would have asked him if he'd rather they stay in bed, talk about nothing for twenty or thirty minutes then see if they could rev up the engines for another round. But that was a couple of nights ago. Since then the novelty had worn off for both of them and she went back to her regular narcotic of reality shows and news programs. She liked "20-20," "Dateline NBC," "Bachelorette" and another program about a bunch of twenty-eight-year-old high school classmates sharing a house together.

She liked to watch television. He had allowed himself to forget that and then remembered it soon after he came to stay with her.

He called out to her from the bedroom.

"Diane!"

"What?" Irritated.

"Is there any gin left?"

She wasn't going to get up and check.

"I don't know, Barry. What do you want me to do?"

He remembered emptying the bottle while they shared a Domino's pizza. Shit.

"Where's the nearest liquor store?"

"The stores close at ten."

"They do?"

"Yeah. State regulation."

"Shit."

"Just — deal with it, Barry. Will you?"

Hell with her, Barry McDermott thought. She always had been a cranky bitch. God, what woman wasn't? He just wanted a drink, that's all. Did she have to carp at him like he was a little boy? It was as if she was mad at him for never marrying her, never treating her like a regular girlfriend. Still mad at him, years after the fact. She had a husband now. A soldier, now stationed in Northern Iraq. Why couldn't she be happy with the situation? Oh. Because the husband wasn't a "professional." She preferred professional men. She had once told him about a guy she had been seeing, a mechanic or something. They had been out on a date and they ran into some friends of his and she could tell that he was embarrassed to be seen in public with her. A sentiment Barry could relate to. "And he wasn't even a *professional,*" she said. Barry had to force himself not to smile then.

Tony Burns, however, was a professional. A dork, but a professional. A lawyer who could run rings around Barry in just about any litigation, but who simply had no understanding of women. Poor Tony. He had tried so hard to hide his love for Diane Creasey, his secretary. But he fooled no one. Not Diane, not Barry. Tony would have married Diane, the poor sap. But like many women who never quite put the seventeen-year-old girl behind them, Diane Creasey could not give her love to a dork. Barry sometimes wondered if he would have ever initiated the affair with Diane if he hadn't known how much Tony the superlawyer desired her. Probably, he would have.

Barry would have preferred to remain in the bedroom and go to sleep, if only to teach Diane a lesson. *I can withdraw too, dammit.* But eventually the smell overpowered the pride and he got out and pulled his underwear and T-shirt on and walked out into the living room. Diane was watching something called "Joe Millionaire." Barry drifted into the kitchen and opened the refrigerator. There was a twelve-pack of Strohs inside. Oh God, Barry thought. Strohs. The husband must have left it here. Barry took one, opened it and shuffled over to the living room couch to take his place. He had seven more beers before Diane went to bed.

Around midnight, he put his pants on and went to his car in the garage. It was an Infiniti G35 coupe. He had bought it six months ago. Next week, the payment would come due. What then? he thought. Did fugitives from the law make car payments? Another thing he had not considered before making his run.

He opened the rear hatch and lifted the cover to the spare tire compartment. The money was still there, as it had been the day before. Eight hundred thousand dollars that he was supposed to be laundering for the British niggers. Motherfucking English neegroes. Smirking at him, ribbing him like he was a jester. He put the cover back on and shut the hatch. He lit a cigarette and tried to think.

Now what? Drive the car to Belize? Who did he know in Belize? What would he do if he got there? Hand over a stack of bills to a realtor and say, I'd like something roomy by the water? He was not an experienced crook. A hardened criminal would know what to do. But he was not a hardened criminal and he did not know what to do. He was a lawyer who had been overwhelmed by cir-

93

cumstances. And it wasn't his fault.

He met Mandy Cranston at a party and presumed she was about seventeen. He called her Mandy Mandy, like the girl in the Barry Manilow song that was popular about twenty years before she was born. Her old man was some sort of cancer surgeon that had more money than the Wrigley brothers. Mandy Mandy was wild, very wild. She asked Barry if he had any coke. Barry said he did and they went to the bathroom where, after things progressed, she snorted a line off his erect penis. They saw each other a few more times after that, usually at his place, and he hadn't really given the whole thing much thought. She never told him she was in love with him. She did tell him that she had been with her high school English teacher, though she did not specify that it had only been a few months before Barry met her.

A few weeks after Barry met her, Mandy Mandy's mother found some crack in her room and confronted her about it. Though she had actually purchased the drugs elsewhere, Mandy Mandy told her mom that she got it from Barry McDermott, attorney at law. The police were called and a bench warrant issued thereafter. At the station, the police informed Barry that Mandy

Cranston was fifteen years old. That's when Barry started crying.

Barry knew the law. Knew that if a girl was a day less than sixteen, consent would not be a defense to statutory rape. It wouldn't matter that Mandy Mandy was as willing as a Barbary Coast showgirl. If the jury believed he had sexual intercourse with her, he would go to prison. And he had done that. Several times.

The fact that he had been arrested at the time he was holding $800,000.00 of Trevor Jim's money was a coincidence. Barry took it as a sign. Providence telling him there was no need to hang around and wait to be convicted.

But trying to stand tall in a tiny garage in Oklahoma City, Barry now wondered if running away had been the right decision. He wondered if he was cut out to be a fugitive. His stomach had been churning since he left Chicago and he had been drinking like a fish. After two days with Diane, he realized he was wearing out his welcome with her. They had never lived together before and now he fully comprehended why. She was getting more and more irritated with him and if the war ended too soon, her husband would return and probably empty his M-16 into the both of them. Even if he did not, she would probably issue some sort of ultimatum to him. Something along the lines of: *Just what have you got in mind, Barry? You gonna marry me? Take me back to Chicago? What are you going to do?*

What were the alternatives?

Stay here.

Look into Belize.

Go home. Get a good lawyer, see if he can get the charges pleaded down to a suspended sentence with the standard rules and conditions of probation. Maybe that could happen. . . .

Look into Mexico . . . then Belize . . . ?

He went back into the living room. The television was still on. There was a cowboy on the screen selling jewelry, saying, "Don't worry if your credit's a little rough around the edges. Heck, everybody's is." For a moment, Barry squinted at the television, trying to make sense of it. Then he picked up the telephone on the coffee table and dialed a number.

Got an answer on the fifth ring.

"Hello?"

"Hello?"

"Barry? Is that you?"

"Yeah."

A pause. Then, "What are you doing?"

"Uh, I'm ah . . . out of town."

"Jesus, God. Where are you?"

"I can't tell you that."

"You left me here alone."

"I know. I'm sorry."

"Jesus."

"I know."

"Just fucking left me here."

"I'm sorry."

"What are you going to do?"

"I don't know yet. I'm thinking of coming back."

"Coming back. For what?"

"I don't know. I can probably cut a decent plea. Or get it dismissed at preliminary hearing. Maybe make a plea."

"Dismissed? What, are you hoping the girl changes her story?"

"I don't know. Maybe."

"Uh, Barry, no offense, but it doesn't sound like you've thought this thing through."

"I know, I know. But I'm working on it. It's complicated, it's complicated."

"No shit. Some guy came by here today, looking for you."

"Who? A cop?"

"No. Not a cop."

"Black guy?"

"No. White guy."

Barry felt his stomach muscles unclench. A little.

"What'd he want?"

"What did he want? He wanted to know where you were."

"What'd you tell him?"

"I told him the truth. I told him I didn't know."

"Yeah . . . ? Did you tell him?"

Cinnamon sighed.

"Barry, you're drunk."

"Huh?"

"When you're drunk, you say 'I'm sorry' a lot. Listen, how can I tell him something I don't know? I don't know where you are."

"I'm in Oklahoma City." He said it quickly, without thought.

Cinnamon pulled up. She said, "Hold on a minute. Let me turn the television off."

Cinnamon put the telephone receiver on the bed. She walked downstairs to the kitchen phone. Barry had a caller i.d. box on that phone. There was a 405 area code number on the screen. Cinnamon wrote it down.

She said, "Why are you telling me now, dummy? The phone could be tapped."

"Is it?"

"I don't know. I didn't tap it. Barry, what are you doing?"

"I don't know, I'm — confiding in you. I'm telling you that I need you and that I miss you."

"Confi— oh, Jesus. Are you trying to get me to ask you to come home? Is that it?"

"No . . . no. I just thought. . . ."

Trailing off now, Barry thought, what? That they had something special together? That somewhere in Cinnamon Barefoot there was the proverbial golden-hearted whore? That the girl he had taken in and clothed and housed would somehow become the Julia Roberts to his Richard Gere? He needed to cut down on the drinking. Still, she was in his house. His home. And she wouldn't even ask him to come back to it. It wasn't working. The phone call, the attempt to create some sort of connection with her, wasn't working. He had not read Cinnamon correctly.

What Cinnamon Barefoot was thinking about was the fifty-dollar bill Evan Maitland had put in her hand. He could give her more, perhaps a lot more, if she could tell him where Barry the child molester was hiding. Pondering it, Cinnamon Barefoot lowered her voice to speak.

"Listen, Barry. You know I miss yah. But whatever you want to do . . . you know."

"Yeah. I know."

Cinnamon said, "Oklahoma City, huh? Is it warm down there?"

"Yeah, it's warmer. Warmer down here. Nice and warm."

"Are you at a hotel?"

"Yeah. I'm at a hotel."

"Liar."

"Look, you don't need to know where I am."

"Okay, Barry, okay." Angry now. "Call me when you get back to town."

Barry said, "I want you out of my house!" But she didn't hear him because she'd already hung up. "You hear me? I want you out! Out, goddammit!"

TWELVE

Two hours after she hung up on Barry and went back to sleep, Cinnamon became aware of an increased light, a presence near her. She opened her eyes and started to sit up in bed. A hand held her down.

Maurice Lee was sitting on the bed. He held a finger to his lips.

"Sssshhh."

Behind, against the door was Richard Lawes. He held a pistol at his side.

Maurice said, "Don't scream. Don't. Scream. We not gyan' hurt you. You scream you make that fellah nervous, he give you somethin' to scream about."

Cinnamon held the sheet above her breasts.

"Just take what you want. I won't say anything."

"We not here to rob you, sis. Your boyfriend, he don't tell you how to set the alarm, huh."

"No, he didn't. He'll be back any minute."

"Be better for you if he were. But I don't think he comin' back anytime soon. He took some money don't belong to him," Maurice said. "But he don't tell you about that, huh."

"I don't know what you're talking about."

"Maybe you don't. You know where he went?"

"He didn't tell me. But I may know where he is."

"Don't play the cat's game with us, sis. You know where he is, you tell us."

"Shit, shit. No wonder."

"No wonder what?"

"There was someone looking for him earlier."

"Yeah, the police, huh?"

"No. I don't think he was a cop. He was a private detective or something."

Maurice looked over his shoulder at Richard then turned back.

"His name," Maurice said.

"Evan something. Maitland. Evan Maitland. He was a prick."

"Maitland, uh. What did you tell him?"

"I told him I didn't know."

"You lie to him, you tell us the truth. That how it is?"

"Wait, wait. Since he left, I found something out."

"What's that?"

"Barry called here a few hours ago. He

was drunk. He's in Oklahoma City. That's in Oklahoma."

"What's he doing there?"

"He's hiding, I guess."

"You got an address?"

"No. I've got a phone number."

She looked into Maurice's eyes. She thought he was kind of good-looking, actually. Good jawline.

She said, "If I gave you the number, you could probably find out the address, couldn't you?"

"Yeah, maybe."

"I'll give it to you for five hundred bucks." She said, "I mean, I don't see why we can't work together on this."

"Yeah, maybe. Maybe I don't let Richard drop you out of the window on your head."

"The number's downstairs on the kitchen counter. You don't believe me, check the caller i.d. yourself."

Maurice gestured to Richard. Richard left the room.

Cinnamon looked into Maurice's eyes. He *was* a handsome man. Cinnamon touched his wrist.

"You don't have to hurt me, you know. I'm not on anybody's side."

Maurice said, "I see that."

Cinnamon leaned forward to kiss him,

letting the sheet drop. But Maurice leaned back. Gently, he pushed her back.

"Easy, sis. That's not what I'm here for."

Maurice had met girls like her before. White fuzzies coming on to the black savage, acting like they were presenting the Zulu with the ultimate prize. He liked women and had no particular bigotry against white women. But when they presumed that, being black, he would naturally welcome any opportunity for golden pussy, it insulted him. A b'woy needed to get laid, but he needed to hold on to his respect too.

Richard returned, holding a piece of paper. He nodded an affirmation.

Cinnamon saw it coming. All she could say was, "You don't have to."

Maurice said, "Sorry, sis." Then he reached for a pillow.

In the car, Maurice said, "I think this Maitland fellah is working for the bondsman."

Richard said, "Why?"

"They call them bail enforcement agents. He bring the fellah back, the bondsman don't lose his money. A bounty hunter."

"Bounty hunter?" Richard liked the sound of it.

"It's not like a western, Richard. He's just a businessman."

"So we got to deal with him now."

"I think he's on his way to Oklahoma now. We got to fly there, get there before he bring Barry back."

"*Cyan* bring guns on the plane."

Maurice nodded.

"Call Trevor Jim, see if he send Jukie there ahead of us. Jukie knows where to get guns anyplace. We'll have to have a car there."

"Can Jukie take care of that too?"

"Jukie's very resourceful."

THIRTEEN

Barry woke up to the sound of Diane clacking around the kitchen. He lay on the couch. He had not returned to the bedroom. Since he had come to her home, it was the first night they had not slept in the same bed. Not a good indication of the status of their relationship. She hadn't asked him to explain it either. If she had, he would have told her it was nothing personal. It was just that her room stunk of cat shit and smoke. The whole house stunk, but the stench was especially concentrated in her bedroom. No, Barry thought. Maybe an explanation wouldn't help. She gave him an uncurious glance now, but did not say anything. She didn't seem angry at him, but there was no warmth in her look either. They were running out of things to say to each other. They had had some good times in the past. She would come over to his house, they would fool around and she would stay the night or she would go home. No big deal either way. But that had been in Chicago. The logistics had been different, less complicated. Now there was this small house that belonged to some soldier and it just wasn't the same. They were not married. They had no family. The sex was good, still, but it wouldn't be enough to get them past the cramped quarters and the stultifying smell. Diane had not yet said anything about him leaving, but that was just a matter of time. It started with silence, that sort of thing. Like now, looking at him blankly, not saying good morning or kissing him goodbye. Not saying much of anything. Just standing there in her blue skirt and ugly blouse. She never had learned to dress, Barry thought. She still wore stonewashed jeans, for godsake, and to see her try to look hip almost made him sad. She looked good naked. But on this morning she had dressed for work. Sometimes there was no avoiding seeing Diane Creasey in clothes.

She said, "Do you mind going to the store for me?"

"No," Barry said. "What do you want?"

"Two-liter bottle of Pepsi. Chips. Maybe some hamburger meat. Buns."

"We still have half that pizza we ordered last night."

Diane frowned. "I don't eat leftovers," she said.

Then she left.

Barry heard the door shut. He lay back on the couch and stared up at the ceiling and wondered if he should just go back to sleep or turn on the "Today" show and see what the temperature was in Chicago. Then he thought, Chicago? What difference does it make what the temperature is in Chicago? Pull your shit together, Barry. Then he heard the engine fire up and he didn't process the sound immediately. The vrroooming whine was a familiar noise. Then he sat up and looked to see Diane's car keys sitting on the kitchen table. She drove a Pontiac GrandAm.

"Oh Jesus, no. Diane!"

She was gone by the time he got to the driveway, the taillights of his G35 fading in the distance.

FOURTEEN

Jukie said, "You don't need to know my name. I need guns and I have money to pay for them."

The fellah with the blonde hair and pock-marked face said, "I like to know who I'm doing business with."

"I told you, you don' need to know."

The pockmarked man said, "I like to know the names of my customers."

Jukie said, "I'm not here to buy no meth, b'woy. I need a car with clean plates and I need guns."

"How many guns?"

"Three pieces. A shotgun too, if you have one."

The pockmarked man said, "Let's see what we can do."

They were in a scrap yard in southern Oklahoma City. Jukie Blake, the Jamaican currently residing in Chicago, Illinois, on duty in Oklahoma. Doing business with a couple of Oklahoma crackers who didn't know what to make of him. A black guy with good clothes and hair pulled back in a pony-tail, must be from Dallas or someplace. The black guy said Russell had recommended them and they knew who Russell was. It would have to be good enough. If the guy had money, it would be fine.

The pockmarked man and another guy he called Jess with a crewcut and glasses stood in the lot, ready to do business. Jukie knew their names and where they could be found if they took a notion to fuck him over and he found it necessary to come back.

Jukie followed them across patches of wet gravel, tiptoeing around little gray pools, until they came to a prefabricated steel building and went inside. There were six vehicles in there, two of them pickups. They led him to an '89 Ford Thunderbird.

Jukie said, "I would prefer a four-door."

"Hold on boy," the pockmarked man said. "I want you to see something."

The pockmarked man opened the driver's side door. He slid his fingers beneath the armrest and then the panel opened up to reveal a small compartment. There were two pistols inside.

"Looky what we got here," the pockmarked man said. "You get pulled over, they ain't gonna find these bad boys. Tailor made for a man like yourself who knows what he wants and knows what he needs to get it done."

Jukie almost smiled at the man. He had nuts, this one. Or he was crazy. "Impressive," Jukie said. "Does the car run?"

"Like a scalded cat."

"Start it for me."

The pockmarked man gestured with his head to the crewcut guy. The crewcut guy got in the Thunderbird and started it. Revved the engine up and down. It sounded healthy.

"Okay," Jukie nodded and the crewcut shut it down.

Jukie said, "The papers are clean?"

"Yeah."

"Show them to me."

Jukie examined the forged documents. They looked good.

"We know what we're doing," the pockmarked man said.

Jukie said, "Yes. Let's see the guns, uh?"

"You're in a hurry, ain't ya," the pockmarked man said. "You got someplace you need to be?"

The airport, Jukie thought. In about forty minutes. But it was none of this *kaffir*'s business. He said, "Three guns. And a shotgun if you have it."

They took him to a Cadillac El Dorado and opened up the trunk. Pulled back a tarp and there they were. Handguns, all sorts.

Jukie said, "I don't see any shotguns."

The pockmarked man looked to the crewcut guy.

"No shotguns?"

The crewcut guy shrugged and held up his hands.

"Sorry, man. No shotguns."

Jukie picked out a 9 millimeter for himself, a .357 revolver and .380 semiautomatic.

"You have ammo for these three?"

"Yeah."

"Okay. How much?"

"Five hundred for the nine, four hundred for the revolver and two fifty for the .380."

"And for the car?"

"The car, that's gonna cost you nine thousand."

Jukie frowned. "That car is fifteen years old," he said.

"And it's clean and equipped for guns."

Jukie sized up the pockmarked little man that was looking at him like he had no shame. He was a funny little man and Jukie was amused by him. He decided to push the fellah a bit, have some fun.

"Are these white prices?" Jukie said.

The pockmarked man smiled.

He said, "Partner, you got me figured all wrong. I'm in business to be in business.

Where money's concerned, why you're just as white as Roy Clark."

Jukie thought, Roy who?

He said, "I give you eight thousand for everything."

"Ahhhh. . . ."

Jukie didn't say anything.

"You got cash?"

Jukie showed him cash, a lot of it.

The pockmarked man said, "Okay, partner. Because I'm nice."

Jukie picked up Maurice and Richard at the American Airlines arrival terminal at Will Rogers Airport thirty minutes later. Maurice looked around the car, saw that it was acceptable. Then he said, "You got guns?"

"Yeah, I took care of everything."

They drove in silence for a while. They reached the interstate and slipped in among trucks and cars in morning traffic. They passed a furniture clearance store, stockyards, a Holiday Inn and a Best Western hotel, billboards advertising Indian casinos and a kid's water park with an enormous blue slide.

From the backseat, Richard said, "Jesus Christ, this is it?"

Maurice said, "Richard thought it'd be a

lot of covered wagons, cowboys and Indians on horses."

Jukie said, "This is America, b'woy. It all the same."

FIFTEEN

"Listen to me," Barry said. "It is very, very important that I talk to her."

"Sir, she is in a closing right now. We can't interrupt her and ask her to take the call."

"You need to tell her that I'm on the phone."

"Who would I say is calling?"

"Barry."

"And your last name?"

"Just Barry."

"Just Barry," the woman on the phone said. "Is this an emergency?"

"Yes, it's an emergency."

"What is it?"

"It's — personal, dammit."

"Sir, I don't like this. You don't tell me your full name and you won't tell me what you want with Diane. You sound like a stalker. We can't get involved in that sort of thing."

"I'm not a stalker, I'm a goddam good friend of hers, goddammit —"

"Sir, you're being abusive. And I don't have to take that."

"Oh, please. Please don't —"

But she had already hung up.

"Fuck!" Barry shouted. What is it with women hanging up the damn phone on him all the time? He was richer now than he'd ever been, a goddam fugitive, and he couldn't even get women to respect him. Receptionists and strippers no less.

He started to dial again, then stopped. Jesus, he had told the woman his first name. If he called her again and gave her the hell she deserved, she'd call the police on him. Some crazy asshole calls himself Barry is threatening to kill Diane. No, no.

He dialed Diane's cell phone.

Got her voice on a recording.

Barry took a breath, then said: "Hey, what's up Diane? Listen, I kinda need the car back. Can you meet me for lunch? Give me a call." He said pretty much the same thing when he called again a half hour later. There was more edge to his voice when he called the third time. The fourth time he called, she answered.

"Barry, I'm at work. What do you want?"

"I want my car back?"

"Why? Are you going somewhere?"

Oh, shit.

"No, honey. I'm not going anywhere. It's just that it's, well, it's my car."

"Sorry I didn't ask. I figured it'd be okay. Are you mad?"

God, patronizing him now. Poor baby.

"No. No. I'm not mad. Just, you know, ask next time. Listen, why don't we meet for lunch? We can switch back."

"It's one-thirty, Barry. I already had lunch."

"Well, can you meet me for coffee?"

"Barry, I'm not going to drive your car to Texas and sell it for parts. What's the matter with you?"

"Nothing, nothing. What time will you be home?"

She let him hear her sigh. "I get off at four-thirty. I'll be home at four-forty-five. Do you want me to stop at a car wash on the way back, vacuum the floorboards?"

"Heh-heh. No. No."

"Okay, then. I'll see you at quarter to five."

Barry felt self-conscious driving the GrandAm. It was an ugly car, built for people Barry felt were lower class and the knowledge that he was in a city where no one, save Diane Creasey, knew who he was brought him little comfort. Like he was wearing a cheap suit. He left the house to buy groceries for Diane. To maintain a scrap of dignity, he made a stop along the way.

He parked the Pontiac at the Red Cup coffeehouse.

The Red Cup was tucked behind a dentist's office with large signs that read: "DO NOT PARK HERE IF YOU ARE A RED CUP CUSTOMER. YOUR CAR WILL BE TOWED." There was a small patio in front of the coffeeshop. To the side there was a goldfish pond against a stone wall, shaded by a couple of trees. Barry ordered a Frappucino and took a seat on the patio. The afternoon sun was warm and he could hear the birds chirping. An oasis in an otherwise ugly part of town.

"Barry?"

He looked up without thinking. And saw a man in casual, expensive clothing holding a coffee to go. White guy in jeans and a red sweater wearing a tan Burberry. Addressing him like he was a classmate from many years back. But the guy didn't look like anyone that had ever been a law student. Barry felt his heart pounding.

"Excuse me?"

"You're Barry McDermott, aren't you?"

"Sorry, guy. I think you've got me mistaken for someone else."

The man remained there, unembarrassed. His direct eye contact unnerved Barry.

"No," the guy said. "I don't think I do. Why don't you show me some identification. Show me I'm wrong."

"Why don't you leave me the fuck alone?"

Maitland put his coffee to go on a table to his right. He kept his eyes on Barry.

"It's time to go home, Barry."

Barry rushed him, throwing his arms around Maitland and shoving him against the table. The table clanked loudly against the wall and customers took notice of the two men grappling. Barry kept his head down and slugged wildly at Maitland's midsection, hitting moderately hard, but not thinking his punches out to points of vulnerability. Frightened and desperate, but inexperienced with real violence.

Using both hands, Maitland forced Barry's head down level with his stomach then brought his knee up sharply into Barry's face. It made a sound like a paddle slapping flat water.

That did it.

Barry cried out and fell to the ground, clutching a bloody face. Groaning at first, twisting on the ground, then sobbing.

The customers were hushed mostly, though one woman started to weep at the

119

sight. Few people enjoy seeing a real fight.

The owner came out.

"What is going on?"

Maitland was bent over Barry, putting handcuffs on his wrists.

"It's okay. I'm a law enforcement officer."

The customers remained still as Maitland packed Barry into the back of his 750iL and drove off. They waited till his car was out of the parking lot before they talked about it.

SIXTEEN

Maitland said, "Tilt your head back."

"You rotten piece of shit. You prick. You broke my nose."

Barry was in the back seat, wailing. It was an unpleasant, uncontrolled sound and Maitland felt embarrassed for him. He looked at Barry in the rearview mirror. Jesus, he might *have* broken his nose. Barry was weak, hopefully sobbing now more out of shame and the anticipation of prison than from pain, and Maitland took no satisfaction in having hurt him. There was blood all over the front of Barry's shirt, maroon stains drying against the yellow cotton. The nose was too fragile. You get a martial arts expert with military training, he can drive the nose up into the man's cerebral cortex and stop him from breathing. Maitland knew the hazards and risks of grown men brawling and had done his best to avoid fights since the ninth grade. He knew that the best thing to do when a loudmouth wanted to start something in a bar was to pay for your drink and walk out. Too much glass in a bar.

Maitland said, "You shouldn't have

rushed me. I mean, what did you think would happen?"

"I thought — I thought maybe you were going to kill me."

"Kill you? Why would I do that?"

Barry looked out the window. His breath slowing now. "I don't know," he said.

They drove by a small stone building with a big model Braum's milk bottle on top.

Barry said, "You're a bounty hunter."

"Hmmm-hum."

"Charlie hire you?"

"Yep."

"How much is he paying you?"

"That's between us."

"Is it the standard ten percent? It is, isn't it? Hey," Barry said, "I'll give you fifty thousand if you let me go."

"Will you."

"No, really. I've, I've got it. I can get it for you today."

"Then I'd be breaking the law."

"Who would know?"

"You would. And then you'd have that over me. We'd be partners, Barry. And I don't like the idea of being partners with the people I'm sent to bring back." He would not speak to Barry McDermott of honesty and the need not to complicate life with corruption because he did not want to discuss such things with him.

Barry said, "Come on. I don't even know your name. That's fifty thousand dollars, tax-free. Tax-free. That's like getting paid *eighty*. You go back to Chicago and tell Charlie you never found me. It's that simple."

"My name is Evan."

"Well, Evan. You seem like a smart guy. You're all right. No, seriously. I'm not mad at you or nothing. You're just doing your job, trying to make a living. Right? But I think you should explore your options here."

Maitland was starting to resent Barry McDermott, talking to him as if he were an insurance adjustor handling a personal injury claim. Lawyers. They could be more insulting than car salesmen.

Maitland made a point of sighing.

"Barry, save your money for your defense."

"Think it out, Evan. You take me back to Chicago, you know I'm gonna sue you. Assault and battery, false imprisonment. I'll sue you for a lot more than the measly thirty thousand Charlie gives you. You can count on that. You let me go, you pocket fifty thousand dollars. Tax-free. The smart choice is obvious."

"You already said the tax-free part. I understood it then." Maitland was coming down from the incident at the coffeeshop and was getting a little bored. He decided to amuse himself.

"So what if you did sue me?" Maitland said. "Would that go to a jury on the civil docket?"

It seemed to push the lawyer back a bit.

"If it didn't settle."

"Oh," Maitland said, "I doubt it'd settle. So we both go before a jury and tell our stories."

"They would side with the truth."

"A child molester? They'd side with that?"

"I didn't molest a child. Goddammit. I did not — have you seen the girl? Have you? She doesn't look a day younger than twenty-five. Jesus, she practically raped me. And if you think I'm the first older man she's been with, you're way wrong."

Way wrong? Maitland thought. Put this man in front of a jury.

Then Maitland pictured himself in court. *Criminal* court, testifying to the self-incriminating statements of this stupid ass. That would be a hassle he could do without.

Maitland said, "Listen, Barry. I think you need to keep your mouth shut about the criminal allegations. The District Attorney will end up asking me to testify against you, and your life's complicated enough as it is."

"You don't know the half of it," Barry said.

Maitland drove in silence. He was through amusing himself for a while.

Barry said, "How did you find me?"

"Your girlfriend's house. You didn't do as good a job hiding as you thought you did."

"Did she turn me in?"

"No. You just didn't do as good a job hiding as you thought you did."

"So you know where she lives?"

"Yeah."

Barry sighed.

"I'm a mess. Can we go back to her house so I can clean up?"

Barry was hoping for a small miracle. He was hoping that if the bounty hunter took him to the house, Diane would be there. And if she was there, his car would be there. And if the car was there, he could show the bounty hunter the money sitting in the trunk. Show him the money. *See? I told you. I wouldn't lie to you, bro. Man, just look at it. Look at all that green.* Ever seen that much in one place? And seeing the money up close and personal, the bounty hunter would go more than a little *Treasure of the Sierra Madre* at the sight. Badges? We don't need no stinkin' badges if the nice lawyer's going to hand him stacks of cash adding up to fifty thousand dollars. It was a hope for Barry. It was all he had.

Maitland didn't see what the man was thinking. He saw a man with blood on his face and shirt. The sight of him could cause problems. Say he pulled up to a stoplight next to a police car. Officer looks over and sees a man that's clearly been beaten . . . then he would have to stop and explain it. That was partly it. He also felt sorry for the man. Barry McDermott was a turd, the kind of man that makes people despise lawyers and a guy that would look at a friend's fifteen-year-old daughter as an opportunity for a pounce. But Maitland was raised in the Catholic Church and had been taught the value of all human life. And as an undercover cop, he had associated with lowlifes from all walks and had come to like some of them. That had been an influence in itself.

He would tell himself later that the decision to take Barry back to the woman's house had been stupid. That it had been motivated in part by an ignorant compassion for a man that probably did not deserve it. He would think later of many things he should have done differently. He would think of them until he persuaded himself not to think of them anymore.

"Okay," Maitland said. "We'll drop by there and let you wash your face and change your shirt. But Barry? You try to rush me again, I'll just shoot you. Okay? I'm through wrestling with you."

Barry's heart sank when they got to the house and his G35 was not in the driveway. But he gripped the hand of hope before letting himself fall off the cliff into utter black, despair. Evan would let him in the house and he could dick around maybe till Diane came home. Playing for time, for minutes. Maybe it could happen in fifteen minutes. He would be standing in front of the bathroom sink and hear the car pull up . . . it could happen. You had to believe.

But the feeling vanished when they walked in the front door and he saw Jukie Blake sitting in Diane's Lazy Boy recliner.

"Hello, Barry," Jukie said. "You've been naughty, huh?"

SEVENTEEN

Barry said, "Hey, Peter."

That was Jukie's name: Peter Blake.

He sat in the living room chair, wearing a slick blue jacket over a black silk shirt. He was a big man, heavy in the chest and shoulders, hair pulled back in a ponytail. His hands rested on the arms of the chair.

There was no gun in sight.

But Maitland kept his eyes on him, sensing danger from this man. Barry had called him by his name, saying "Peter" in a way that gave away his terror. Maitland slipped his hand into his coat pocket, felt his fingers on the butt of his .38 snub.

He saw the man Barry called Peter studying him.

The man said, "Are you Mr. Maitland?"

"I am."

"Why don't you take your hand out of your pocket. I'm a friend of Barry's."

Maitland said, "He doesn't seem too happy to see you."

"Course he is. I'm one of his clients."

"How is it you know my name?"

"We are informed."

"Who is we?"

"That is not your business."

"This man is my prisoner. That's my business." Maitland said, "What do you want with him?"

"We just want to talk to him."

"Go ahead."

"Privately."

"He's going back to Chicago. You can visit him in county jail, talk to him then."

"Hey," Jukie said. As if to say there was no need to be rude. "Work with me, mon. I have things to discuss with him, too."

"You're Jamaican."

"What of it?"

"And you're not from here."

"Like I told you, I am a client of Barry's."

"He's in trouble with the law. You may want to get another attorney."

In a tone that neither Maitland nor Barry liked, Jukie said, "We want this one."

Peter "Jukie" Blake was twenty-nine years old and as he sat in Diane Creasey's living room he had killed seven men. Five in Kingston, two in Chicago. He had considered the killings warfare. He was intelligent and, as Maurice had said, resourceful. He was likable too, in his own way. There were a handful of Gang Task Force cops in Chi-

129

cago that even liked him. They thought he
could have been a successful salesman outside of a life of killing and crime. The Task
Force agents were, like most all cops, right-
wing Republicans; but even they believed
that Jukie's having grown up in a country
that knew so much bloodshed was largely
responsible for making him a menace to society.

Jukie kept his hands on the arms of the
chair as he regarded the white bounty hunter
in front of him. He regarded Maitland as a
man not to be hated, but simply as a man. He
had a job to do, a means of making a living as
he had to do. A bounty hunter here in the
west, almost certainly with a gun in his coat
pocket. Jukie had a 9 millimeter in his right
jacket pocket. He could draw on the fellah
now, maybe beat him to it. But the fellah
looked ready for that. Even so, Jukie
thought, anyone can shoot. Few can negotiate an agreement.

Jukie said, "How much is he worth to
you?"

Maitland said, "Thirty thousand dollars."

"Mr. Maitland, I'm going to be straight
with you because you strike me as being a
man of reason and good sense. He is worth
more than that to us. We can give you
more than that. All you have to do is turn

around and walk away."

"And then you'll kill him."

"And what would that be to you? He is a man that molests little girls. He is not worth defending."

"I'm not defending him."

"You are protecting him. And he is not worth that either. What he is worth, to us, is forty thousand dollars. Why are you smiling?"

"He gave me a better offer."

Jukie smiled then, showing strong teeth. He looked at Barry.

"That right? You very generous Barry, with our money."

Maitland said, "He stole from you?"

"Yeah, that's right. He stole from us."

"How much?"

Jukie shook his head. "Don't worry about that. He is a thief too."

"Intriguing," Maitland said.

"Yes," Jukie said. "Hey."

"Yeah."

Jukie pointed a finger at Maitland. "I bet you used to be a policeman."

"That's right."

"But no more, uh? I tell you something: we are like a police force too, in our way. This fellah has broken the rules. He has be-haved badly and he must answer for it. Do

131

you understand that?"

"Sure."

"So you'll leave him with us?"

"No."

"Mr. Maitland, be reasonable. You want to make a livin'? I respect that. But like Clint say in that movie, dyin' ain't much of a livin', bwoy."

"I think you watch too many movies."

Jukie Blake shook his head, showing disappointment.

"Mr. Maitland, you don't know what you getting into. Take what I am offering you and go home."

"I'm afraid I can't do that."

Jukie frowned and Maitland focused on his eyes and his hands and got ready to tell Barry to back out of the front door. He would walk backward all the way to the car because this guy was not someone you could take your eyes off. And then the front door clicked open and it couldn't have been Barry opening it because Barry was still standing off to his left, hands cuffed to a chain around his belly. Maitland looked at the belly chain, thinking, I can probably take that off now, while the sixth sense made him turn and look at two black guys come in the house and his heart jumped as he stepped back trying to focus on the guys coming in and Jukie at the same time, but his vision was not panoramic and Jukie moved quickly, taking a black metal object out of his jacket pocket as Maitland said, "Don't!" and took the .38 snub out of his coat pocket and Jukie fired at him. Maitland fired one shot back but felt the punch in the right side of his chest, knocking back against the bedroom door, knocking it open and knocking him on the floor.

Things went into quick and slow motion then. Lying on the bedroom floor, Maitland kicked the door shut. Heard someone push against it and kicked it shut again. He still felt the effect of the punch in his chest and he knew it was bad, bad, bad, but he pointed the snub up at an angle to the figure behind the door and fired into it three times. Heard a man grunt and collapse on the other side. Knew that he had one shot left in the little gun and was thinking about what to do when a barrage of gunfire came through the door.

Maurice put his attention on the bedroom door and Barry ran for the front door. He got to it, but Jukie saw him and shot him three times in the back. Barry slumped against the door and then to the floor.

Maitland crawled to a spot about ten feet from the bedroom window, then took a desperate professional wrestling dive right through it. He landed outside and felt the cold against his sweat and he got up and ran. Fell and got up and ran again, behind the house then behind the backyard of the house. Into an ugly wooded area near a viaduct. Ran until he fell again and then he couldn't get back up. He lay on his back, looking up at the dark brown trees set against the cold winter sky, and the white blurred and then became black.

EIGHTEEN

The dashboard in Barry's car had warm green lighting illuminating the speedometer and tachometer. Red lighting showing what station the tuner was on. The darkness was interrupted by a flash of blue and red. Blue and red. The shadows played on the woman's face in the car, her eyes widening at the scene.

Diane slowed, and then stopped the car.

Police vehicles in her driveway and on the street. She saw neighbors standing in their front yards with their arms folded.

Unconsciously, Diane backed the car away from the house before parking it. Looking at the uniformed patrol officers talking with a black plainclothes cop, she locked the G35. Then walked toward them.

"Excuse me," she said. "I live here."

"What's your name, ma'am?" the uniformed officer said.

"Diane Johnson."

The black cop said, "Get Detective Hunnicut."

Detective Rick Hunnicut was as big as the

135

black detective. He had blonde hair, cut close, his face pitted, the scars of steroid use when he played football for Oklahoma University. One and a half years before he got cut from the team, though he let people think he'd played for four. A Sooner during the bleak post-Switzer era but long before Stoops came on board and redeemed the sports talk radio shows. No one remembered him or his teammates, veterans of the ignoble Gibbs regime. But he swaggered nonetheless. Rick Hunnicut was not really a stupid man, but he was a mediocre detective because he didn't pay attention to people and things and he spent too much time focusing on his own presentation.

Detective Hunnicut stood over Diane Creasey Johnson with the intent of intimidating her.

He said, "You say you live here?"

"I do live here. My husband and I."

"And who might he be?"

"Jeff Johnson."

"Where is he now?"

"He's in Iraq. He's a soldier."

"Well, now. Is he home on leave?"

"No."

"You sure about that?"

The detective seemed to be smiling. A shitty, cold smile.

"I think I'd know."

The blonde detective led her into the house and to the corpse of Barry McDermott. He had been shot four times, once in the head and three times in the back. It was a mess, like someone had shoved an M-80 into a cantaloupe and lit the fuse. Chunks of brain matter and skull spread out, blood staining the wood floor like spilt wine.

For a brief moment, it seemed unreal. But then Diane recognized the watch on Barry's wrist and she screamed.

The detective took her outside.

"Ssshhh, sshhh," he said, creeping her out. He made it worse when he put his arm on her shoulder. "Calm down, now. Calm down. Miss Johnson, who is he?"

"He's —"

"Huh?"

"He's a friend."

"Uh-huh. A close friend?"

Diane sniffed. "I guess."

"Did your husband know?"

Diane reached for the strength to fight this big prick and didn't find it.

"No," she said. "He didn't know."

"How do you know he didn't know?"

"He's in Iraq. He doesn't know anything."

The black detective, whose name was Lewis, caught the significance of the remark. But he kept quiet. Hunnicut was lead detective.

Hunnicut said, "Ms. Johnson, did you know you were harboring a fugitive?"

"Harboring a what? What are you talking about?"

"I'm talking about the dead man in your living room."

"Barry, a fugitive? He's a lawyer. Not a criminal."

"He was a wanted man, Ms. Johnson. He skipped bond in Chicago."

"What?"

"You didn't know? He raped a little girl back home."

Hunnicut made direct eye contact with Diane after that, as if to say, how do you like them apples, mama?

But didn't get the horrified reaction he'd hoped for. Diane Johnson *née* Creasey rolled her eyes.

"Well, good grief," she said. She sighed before she spoke again. "Who shot him, then? The girl's father?"

Hunnicut was put off balance by her nonchalance. He looked at Detective Lewis briefly, recovering, then said, "We don't know yet. We got a guy we need you to take a look at. His identification says he's from Chicago too."

"Yeah? Where is he?"

"He's at the hospital."

Diane sighed again. She said, "Is this gonna take long?"

NINETEEN

Before Tina Roberts hooked up with Dr. Brahms she thought he was like a lot of white men she had known, wanting to make love to her because he wanted the exotic experience of being with a black woman. A new experience to share with his friends or put down in his own book of carnal conquests. *Black chick, check. Now, where do I find a Chinese girl?* She was a good-looking woman, Tina. Tall and long-legged with nice skin, and any number of white boys had come on to her, looking to get Christie Love. Tina was in her late thirties, just old enough to remember the television show. She had vague memories of a sexy mama, in a caftan and thick afro, karate chopping some dude in the neck before sending him over the balcony of her high-rise apartment. But Tina Roberts didn't grow up to be a private detective. She became a nurse.

At Baptist Hospital she met Gerhard Brahms, M.D. From Aachen, Germany, and looking about as Aryan as a man could look. Blonde-haired, blue-eyed, tall and broad-shouldered — a poster boy for the master race.

Gerhard was about her age, single and a little different. He asked her out to dinner a few weeks after they met. She said no and he was cool about it. "Some other time, perhaps." And respected her decision.

But they grew closer after that, would chat during breaks, and she came to see that he wasn't looking for the sexual diversity kick but respected her and actually listened to what she had to say. Eventually, they had dinner at a nearby Mexican restaurant and she invited him back to her house. They made love that night, pretty much at her instigation. Lying on top of her after, he said, "I want to see you again." And meant it.

She said, "But it's complicated." Thinking not only of the cultural differences and explaining this descendant of the Reich to her family, but also about the fact that they worked together. Surgeon and scrub nurse, standing with each other at the operating table all day then coming home to the same place at night. Like a lot of relationships that begin in the workplace, it would become an instant marriage.

But Gerhard had said, "Why should it be complicated?" He was direct in communication. Not impolite, necessarily; he simply said things without leading up to them. She liked that about him.

That had been months ago and to her surprise, it seemed more simple than anything. Eventually, she allowed him to acknowledge their relationship openly at the hospital. It led to raised eyebrows and whispers in the corridors to be sure, but that sort of thing did not concern Dr. Brahms. He was a very talented surgeon and the staff felt he was entitled to a certain amount of what they considered eccentricity. Some likened him to Christian Barnard, the South African doctor that had performed the first heart transplant and had been on the Oklahoma Baptist staff years earlier, though Gerhard thought the comparison was simplistic and mildly insulting to both him and Barnard.

On a cold evening in late January, Gerhard Brahms removed a lung from the man who was brought in with a gunshot wound. A nine-millimeter bullet had gone in the man's chest, tumbled around inside and flipped out of his back. He had been found in a wooded area in north Oklahoma City. Leaves and deadfall had stanched the flow of blood and probably saved his life. Nurse Roberts assisted Dr. Brahms in the surgery.

After they cleaned up, they sat in the cafeteria drinking coffee.

Tina told him the hospital administrator said the police wanted to talk to the man.

Gerhard shrugged.

"He was in a gun battle."

Tina said, "He's not from here, apparently. He's from Chicago."

"Really."

"You ever been to Chicago?"

"No."

"We should go there sometime."

"It's cold, uh?"

"Yeah, it's cold. But it's nice. We could go in the spring when it's warmer. There's a baseball park there called Wrigley Field. It's beautiful."

"Baseball?"

"You might like it."

"Maybe."

"Give it some thought, Gerhard. We need to see what we're like outside of our small world of house and hospital."

"I'm not worried about that," he said.

The hospital administrator stood with Dr. Brahms in the hall, asking him to "summarize the status" of the gunshot patient on the fourth floor. The hospital administrator was short and stocky and looked like a nun. She was fifty years old and had retained, to her detriment, those earnest qualities that had once made her a very good student. Her name was Shirley Rice and she had an imperious manner and was not popular with the staff. Shirley sensed their dislike for her and tried to make up for it by telling sex-related emergency room stories. Show she was one of the gang. It didn't work; the emergency room staff had long since grown used to patients with golf balls up their asses and they could sense that Shirley was trying too hard. She was no more into dark humor than Kathie Lee Gifford, and it showed. Gerhard felt sorry for her, so he treated her with respect and looked her in the eye when he spoke to her. Because of this, she grew to rely on him more than a manager should and he became a sort of mediator between her and the people that answered to her. Gerhard didn't welcome the role, but being of a philosophical bent, told himself that they were all in this together.

Gerhard Brahms said, "He's conscious now. The surgery went okay. His lung was collapsed when he got here. I tried to save it, but the bullet tumbled before it went out of his back. There was too much damage to the lung, so I had to remove it. We should be able to dismiss him the day after tomorrow."

Shirley said, "He was covered, right?"

"Uh, yes. Prudential, I think." Gerhard

let it pass. He said, "He was a policeman, yes?"

"No. He was not a policeman. He's from Chicago."

"Okay."

"The police want to question him. The Oklahoma City police."

"Yes."

"I think we should allow them to do it. I think we have to allow them to do it."

"What did they tell you?"

"They said they want a statement from him."

"Do they have a warrant, papers?"

"No. But — they're police officers. And he was involved in a shooting. They seem all right. Straight shooters."

"I'm his treating physician."

"Right." She acknowledged him. "I understand that."

TWENTY

Diane found the money the next day.

She knew he had something in his car that he was worried about because she had never seen him get so nervous about his possessions. So she thought there was probably something in the car that was making him apeshit. She thought it would be drugs, a brick of cocaine in the trunk that he was going to sell later. But it turned out to be about $800,000.00.

What the hey?

Where did he get all this money?

Did he steal it? If he did, it would explain why he left Chicago in such a hurry. The creep. He never told her the truth about anything. To him, she was merely the in-between warm place to put it when he didn't have another girlfriend. The humiliating pattern had become undeniably clear back when she was in Chicago. But she had pretended to forget it and started that stupid e-mail correspondence with him. It was her fault, she thought. She had allowed herself to believe that he had changed, had changed his feelings for her. But he hadn't. He was still a creep, but now he had gotten weird too.

No, not weird. Maybe just paranoid. Because he had all this money.

He must have stolen it. A man like Barry didn't make that kind of money. He made enough to buy nice things, but he had never handled a class action case, never gotten the multi-million dollar pop on a medical malpractice case. In fact, he did what he could to avoid trying cases. What Barry the attorney did was look good as an attorney.

Who had said that? The part about Barry looking good and dressing well, but not knowing how to try a case. Tony. Tony Burns had said it. Poor Tony.

Poor Tony? What about me? she thought. What about me? What do I do with all this money?

Call Detective Hunnicut, tell him about it.

No. He was an asshole. Besides, he didn't seem to know anything about it.

Call Jeff, her husband. Tell him we're rich.

Yeah . . . bull*shit*. She hadn't married him for those sorts of reasons. She had married him because she was tired of not being married. He was an okay guy. A bit of a bore, but decent in the sack and he had a steady

147

job. Besides, down in this dump no one had to know who he was. She could hide her non-professional husband.

Professional men. They would sleep with her, say, oh you're good, baby, oh you're good, you know how to do it, do it, do it, I want you, I want you, give it to me . . . blah, blah, blah. Then she'd find a wedding ring in the glove compartment or, worse, get a telephone call from a wife asking why she had sent a Valentine's Day card to their home. Assholes, users, creeps.

Barry hadn't been married. Well, most of the time he hadn't been married. But he wasn't much better. Great in bed, to be sure. And funny, and sometimes fun. But still a creep and a pussy.

That night, Diane Johnson took a long look at her life and the small house she was living in and decided she didn't want to be Diane Johnson anymore. In fact, she wasn't even sure she wanted to be Diane Creasey anymore. She did decide she wanted to go back to Chicago, rent a nice apartment on the Gold Coast and get out of this cowtown.

She took the money out of Barry's G35 and put it in a suitcase and slid it under her bed. The next day, she called in sick at work and drove the G35 to a downtown parking garage. She waited until she couldn't see anybody, then removed the license plates from the car and put them in a bag. She threw the plates into a trash Dumpster and took a bus back to the house.

Two days after that, she drove back to Chicago.

TWENTY-ONE

He had been off the oxygen tank for a day and a half now and every breath hurt, like he'd fallen asleep in front of a rolling tractor tire. The previous night had been his first without morphine and he had spent much of it awake, moaning uncontrollably, sweating and shaking. Sleep came only through sheer exhaustion and even then it was short-lived. Still, he sensed it would not be pleasant and, being a former cop himself, he knew that positioning and body language were important to the psychology of the interrogation. So he struggled out of bed and into a checkered bathrobe. Using the walker, he maneuvered over to the window and leaned against the ledge. He would not lie down as they stood on opposite sides of him and told him all the laws he had violated and what a dumbshit he had been.

When the police came, he stood — hollow eyed, pale and weak. But standing.

Two big-shouldered cops, with the serious expressions, telling him they were going to be hard-ons. The black guy said his name was Detective Ed Lewis, Jr. and seemed almost human. The other one introduced himself as Rick Hunnicut. He had blonde hair and a mustache. He took the weak suck of a man in, smiled coldly and said, "You look like you've been rode hard and hung up wet."

"Really," Maitland said. "I thought I'd been shot."

It put the blonde detective back on his heels a bit. A smart-ass, he thought. But he ain't too damn smart, leaning on a walker like an old woman.

"Why don't you just tell us what happened," Hunnicut said. "Maybe you'll feel better after you do."

Maitland told them. The truth mostly, leaving out the part about kneeing Barry in the face because these two seemed like the type of cops that would second-guess him on that. *That sounds excessive. Did you have to use physical force? That sounds like excessive force to me. I think there were things you could have done before taking it to that level.* And so forth. Cops are never more unforgiving when they're going after other cops. Or ex-cops. Maitland took his time with it, shifting eye contact between Detective Lewis and Detective Hunnicut. At times Hunnicut would stick his finger in his ear and look off with one of those give-me-a-fucking-break expressions. Maitland resisted the urge to poke him in the chest with a leg of the walker and spoke until he was finished.

Which would have been the part about him passing out somewhere behind Diane Creasey's house.

Detective Lewis said, "Then what happened?"

"I told you, I passed out. I remember vaguely riding in the ambulance, but that's it."

Hunnicut said, "You don't remember anything else, huh?" Sarcastic tone, talking to Maitland as if he were a country meth dealer or a child.

"No, Detective, I don't."

"Why don't you tell us what really happened?"

"I just told you."

"No you didn't. You left some things out. You left a lot out."

"Why don't you tell me what I left out, Detective? And then we'll both know."

"Okay, son, I will. We have trouble believing you just happened to run into those Jamaicans. We think you knew them." Hunnicut left it there, wanting to see if it would cause some alarm.

"You think I knew them. How would I know them?"

"You're from Chicago."

"So what?"

"Boy, you a tough guy, huh. But you're not smart. You say you shot one of them through a door. Where is he?"

"How should I know? If he's alive, he left. If he's dead, they probably carried him out of there. The Jamaicans aren't known for being stupid. Am I the only one you found?"

"Yeah," Detective Lewis said. "You and McDermott."

"Well, do you think I made them up?"

"No," Hunnicut said. "They're real, all right. We just think you're lying about not knowing them."

Maitland could sense where this was going, but he said, "Why would I know them?"

And saw Hunnicut's shitty smile.

Hunnicut said, "We checked you out, son. This's not the first time you've done business with drug dealers. Is it?"

Maitland frowned. "I see," he said. "Who did you speak to?"

"We spoke to Chicago."

Maitland said, "When you spoke to Chicago, did his name, by chance, happen to be Lieutenant Terry Specht?"

The black detective's expression revealed that it was.

And Maitland, an experienced interrogator himself, said, "You did, didn't you?"

"Yeah," Hunnicut said, "we talked to Lieutenant Specht. He told us about a drug dealer named Ronnie Ellis. In Cabrini Green. You took money from Ellis and then you killed him."

"Well, I killed him all right. Shot him twice in the chest. I didn't take his money, though."

"Why did you kill him?"

"He was trying to kill me."

"You say."

"Yeah, I say. I said it before a board of review, under oath. And again before an arbitrator at my hearing. They believed me. No criminal charges were filed. You want to see the transcripts of the hearings, I can have them faxed to you."

"I don't need to see them."

"Why not? Would it interfere with the conclusion you've already formed?"

"The fact that you got some outside party to believe your bullshit at an arbitration don't mean nothing to me."

"Well, it meant a lot to me. It meant I got my job back and got my pension restored."

"You didn't stay. You quit six months after that."

"That's right."

"How come?"

"I didn't want to work there anymore."

"More money in the private sector, uh?"

"No. Not necessarily. What did Terry tell you?"

"Lieutenant Specht told me that you were on the take and that Ronnie Ellis was the chief witness against you and you knew it. You were a narcotics officer that took pay-offs and Ellis was about to flip on you. So you killed him."

"Yeah, I figured Terry would tell you something like that. Well, Lt. Specht had an interesting theory and he testified about it at the arbitration. But the arbitrator didn't buy it. No one with any sense did. Anyway, the arbitrator ordered the Department to reinstate me with back pay. And let me tell you, Detective, it was *just* that easy."

Maitland snapped his fingers on *just*.

It was intended to rattle the toothy detective and it did. Hunnicut came toward Maitland, tense, like he was going to punch him in the chest or pull his walker away.

"What are you doing?"

A voice, authoritative and sharp. German.

The detectives turned to see Dr. Brahms, a man less big than them. But sure of himself and on his own turf.

Hunnicut answered him.

"We're conducting an investigation, Doctor. We'll just be a little while longer."

"It looks to me like you were about to assault my patient."

"Doctor, this is our business."

"And this man is my patient. Get out now or I'll report you to your superiors."

"Are you threatening a law enforcement officer, Doctor?"

"Yes. For breaking the law."

"Doc, you want to get shitty with us we can come back here with a court order."

"Bring it then," Dr. Brahms said. "I'll pass it on to the administrator."

Detective Lewis felt his heart beating. It had become a scene now, out in the open, and he feared if they stayed any longer Hunnicut would open up a can of O.C. spray on this doctor's face and get both their asses hauled before their own internal affairs review board. He touched Hunnicut on the arm.

"Let's go," he said.

They walked past the surgeon and out of the room. Brahms stared straight ahead, not at Maitland. From the hall, they heard Hunnicut say, "Fuckin' Nazi." Their footsteps drifted away.

Maitland said, "Sorry."

But the German shook his head, telling him to forget it. He had dignity, this one.

And a certain amount of style. Maitland could see him holding his own in other venues.

Dr. Brahms said, "We need to talk."

TWENTY-TWO

Brahms said, "Are you a runner?"

"No."

The doctor nodded. "Do you smoke?"

"Sometimes."

"Not anymore. Not for a while anyway."

"Well, yeah."

"I am a realist, Mr. Maitland. I will speak bluntly. You will not grow another lung. You will forever have half the breathing capacity you had before. You will be in pain, a lot of pain, for at least another week. Did you sleep last night?"

"Not much."

"Good. Morphine is habit-forming, Mr. Maitland. The sooner you wean yourself off it, the better. I have prescribed Percocet. It will help some, but I want you to cut the dosage in half next week. That can be habit forming as well. Painkillers can be very addictive."

"I know. I was a narcotics officer for — before."

Maitland thought he saw the doctor tilt his head; perhaps he'd heard the detectives earlier.

"You were lucky, sir. The bullet passed through your chest and lung and went out through the back. Often when a person is shot through the chest there is damage to the brachial plexus. This generally causes permanent nerve damage; your right arm would never really work again."

Maitland flipped through his mind's encyclopedia and rested on an entry for Bob Dole. Chest wound at nineteen, spending the next fifty years holding a pen in one hand . . . losing to Clinton, then making commercials for Viagra. Jesus.

The doctor said, "The point is, this did *not* happen to you. Whether or not you are a religious man, it is important to focus on the positive. Do you understand?"

"I understand."

"I tell you that because it will be at least six months before you begin to feel remotely normal again. It is not unusual to suffer depression over this. That is why I caution you about the painkillers. But you are a relatively young man and the body can be remarkably adaptable."

Maitland thought about saying, "Strength through joy, eh?" Then realized he was as bigoted as Hunnicut and kept it to himself. A relatively young man. Bullshit. He was pushing forty, probably seven or eight years older than the doctor giving him these clipped words of solace. He would be depressed later. Right now he was pissed off and a little frightened.

"There is a general in your armed forces, led a battalion in Iraq. He too was shot in the lung in that other war, ten years ago. Like you, he had his lung removed. Now at the age of fifty, he can do more pushups than any nineteen-year-old private in his regiment."

"That's comforting."

"It's something, Mr. Maitland."

Maitland looked out the window. Cars moving up and down the Northwest Expressway, a green SUV slowing, then turning into the drive for the Borders bookstore . . . a soccer mom, perhaps, meeting a friend for coffee. The sun glaring down on ground that had warmed during his stay in the hospital. Seasons changing.

"Yeah," Maitland said. "I suppose it is. Thank you. For everything."

They shook hands and the doctor left Maitland to his bed. Maitland never saw him again.

TWENTY-THREE

Jukie said, "Is nobody's fault, mon."

Trevor Jim frowned.

"How is that?"

"Mon, is like a natural disaster. He show up, he start shooting."

"That's not what you said. You said you tried to negotiate with him."

They were in Trevor Jim's condominium on Lake Shore drive. Twelve floors up, overlooking the green of Lincoln Park and the blue of Lake Michigan.

Jukie sat in a leather chair. Trevor Jim was taking the Dylan CD out of the player and putting it in its case. Then he started looking for another, his back to Jukie.

The music was off and they could hear the sound of the south wind pushing itself against the building.

Jukie said, "Yeah, I try to deal with him. He's a man, isn't he? I think he wants money and to avoid a shooting like anyone would."

"But he don't trust you. He thinks you just playing him, get him to drop his guard and then you shoot him. Now I got to call

Richard's mother, tell her her son is dead."

"It just happened. Listen, we got Barry. That's the main thing."

That they did. But lost Richard. They had to take his corpse out and bury it in another spot, twenty miles away. Maurice said a prayer afterwards.

"You killed Barry, bredda. You killed him before finding out where he hid my money. You think that's a good thing?"

Jukie said, "Mon, be reasonable. All right, Richard is dead. I'm not happy about it either. But I do the job, mon. Barry not around to tell the police what he knows about you. That has been taken care of."

"Yeah, but I still don't have my money."

"There wasn't time. The police were coming; we heard the sirens. What you expect me to do? Now I can't speak for you, maybe you a much braver fellah than me. But when I do some killing in a place I don't live, I think it's a good idea to get out of there afterwards."

"You should have shot Mr. Maitland the second he walked in the door. And you should have let Barry live until he told you where the money was. You did it wrong both ways."

Jukie sighed.

"Barry almost got out the front door. I had to shoot him."

"Did you."

"Mon, you were not there."

"I know if I had been, I'd've got the money."

But he had not been there, Jukie thought. Trevor Jim thought he was immortal, that had he been there it'd've all been milk and honey and easy pussy. But he hadn't seen the fellah with the gun and the look on his face. A killer, a soldier. Something about him. Jukie didn't think Richard was the first man Maitland had killed.

Trevor Jim found what he wanted — Steppenwolf — and put it in the player. He turned and said, "Hey, you okay with me, Jukie. But I don't think you seeing my side of it. You talk as if we lucky or something. But that Maitland fellah, he still alive. He saw you and Maurice. And I still don't have my money."

"Maybe so," Jukie said. "But I say the best thing to do is leave it alone."

"Leave it alone? Mon, you not making no sense. He's got to die. Soon."

Jukie understood the logic of what Trevor was saying. It didn't make sense. But there were senses beyond sense. There was bad karma, bad vibes that had come with this thing. He knew it and felt it. But he also knew that if he tried to explain it to Trevor Jim, the Indestructible, Trevor Jim would intimate that he was just afraid, less than a man. Maybe even kill him for cowardice. Trevor. Jukie thought of him now as Trevor. Not Trevor Jim now, but just Trevor. A man, like any other. Except Trevor had bought into all that *Harder They Come*, Jimmy Cliff, rebel-outlaw code of vengeance bullshit. It was all a dream, fool. At the end of the movie, Cliff missed the boat and then he got killed.

Trevor said, "You don't have to do it, if that's what concerns you."

"I can do it tonight, mon. You know that. But there are better ways."

"Go see Frank then," Trevor Jim said. "He do it for you. Fix it, Jukie."

TWENTY-FOUR

They left the sun in Oklahoma. Around Joplin it became overcast and by Springfield it was bleak and gray. The Ozark Mountains flashing past them, trees not yet budding.

Bianca said, "You feeling any better?"

Maitland stirred in the passenger seat. He could walk now, with the use of a cane. But like most people that have undergone traumatic surgery, he felt like he had been stampeded by a herd of elephants. Hurt, depressed, missing the morphine.

"No."

Bianca wanted to reach out and touch him. Squeeze his hand or touch his knee. But she didn't. She looked him over and returned her attention to the road. Ninety miles to St. Louis and another four and a half hours after that. She had the 750iL on cruise control, eighty-five mph, though the V-12 made it feel like they were going fifty. There were billboards advertising Branson entertainers. Bianca didn't recognize any of them.

Evan wasn't looking so good. Not broken, exactly. But battered to be sure. Pale and weak, writhing in his seat, sweating in the cold. Like he was going through some sort of withdrawal, which he was.

She had flown to Oklahoma City the night before and stayed the night in the small hotel the hospital had built. She picked up Maitland's car from the police pound and wrote out a $140.00 check to do it. Then picked Evan up from the hospital. He was dressed and ready to go when she first saw him. She wondered if he did not want her to see him in his hospital room, but didn't ask him about it.

But he's not your husband, she thought.

She wondered why she should think such a thing. Bianca was not a religious woman. But she knew something about the world, something about adultery. She knew that it did not start with two people getting into bed with each other. That it started long before that. It was what it was. Americans, she thought, were funny about sex and adultery. They made a carnival about going after a president that got some fat girl to service him under a desk. And the man, in turn, replied that he had not had sex with her. By sex, apparently he had meant intercourse. A distinction which didn't make an ounce of sense to her. She had not been to Catholic confession since she was a little

166

girl in Milano, but she would agree with the most dogmatic priest in Scranton that an open mouth kiss was as much a betrayal as a full-blown lay. She had discussed *l'affaire* Clinton once with Evan and said, "But what is it he did wrong?"

"I don't know," Evan had said. "He had an affair with a young girl."

"But that's between him and his wife. Why they want to put him in jail?"

"They don't want to put him in jail."

"It looks like they do."

"No . . . look, he lied about it."

"You are *supposed* to lie about it."

"Bianca —"

"He lied to her, is that the problem?"

"No. He lied under oath."

"About the girl?"

"Yeah."

"Was he in court or something?"

"Kind of."

"Was it a divorce case?"

"No."

"Then why would they ask him a question like that?"

"I don't know, Bianca. Do we have to talk about it?"

"Is adultery, uh?"

"Yeah, it's adultery."

"That's not illegal here, is it?"

167

She remembered, when she first moved to the States, being surprised to learn that prostitution was illegal.

"No, it's not illegal. Don't be silly."

"Then why is he in trouble?"

Maitland had sighed and retreated to his newspaper.

"I don't know, Bianca."

She had wanted to ask Evan something else, but he was irritated with the subject. She wanted to ask, "But why didn't he fuck her?" Though she wouldn't have used the word *"fuck"* in front of him. Or maybe she would have. Maitland was an American too and parochial in his way. He said the word all the time, but for some reason would be bothered if she said it in the sense that it was intended. Americans were . . . strange about such things. They committed adultery, like any other species, but seemed to make such a big thing about it. Or maybe they didn't make enough of a big thing about it. Where she came from, it happened, but people didn't necessarily divorce over it. Still, she believed that they took affairs more seriously. She believed that Americans liked to marry because they were in love. Or liked to think they were. The product of too many Julia Roberts movies and television shows with Paul Reiser and Helen Hunt. And

168

when they realized, inevitably, that mar-riage wasn't quite . . . like . . . that . . . they had trouble accepting it. So instead of taking a lover for a few months and seeing that another man or woman wasn't all that terrific, they would get a divorce and, usu-ally within a very short time, take another spouse. And they went after their leader be-cause he didn't have sexual intercourse with a sad, unsophisticated girl. It didn't make sense.

Once, she had thought about going to bed with Evan. On a night when they were working late and she knew her husband was out of town, she suddenly looked at him smiling at a customer and thought, *I could.* Then it became, *I'd like to.* But he was her friend. And she loved her husband. And she knew it would change everything.

So she put it away. And when she got home that night and shut the door behind her to an empty house, she felt relieved.

Watching him lie back on the reclining car seat, shivering and sweating, she won-dered now if she had taken it back out. Not a desire for him, exactly. But a feeling of closeness. Maybe it was worse than lust. Still, he was a man. A human being. And whether or not she felt ambivalence about her feelings toward him was probably meaningless to him right now. He looked like the only thing he was feeling was shitty.

"Evan," she said. "I think we need to stop for the night, uh?"

Maitland turned toward her, maybe to see if she meant anything by it. Then looking like he didn't really care either way.

"Okay."

She pulled the car into a Motel 6 in Lebanon. Using his credit card, she checked them into a room on the ground floor. She helped him from the car into the room, got his coat and shoes off and eased him down on the bed.

Outside it was getting colder. Five in the evening, with darkness coming in. There were only three other vehicles in the parking lot. The swimming pool white and empty.

Maitland was asleep in minutes. Bianca lit a cigarette and sat on the opposite bed. She left the television off and could hear the sounds of traffic thrumming by on the interstate. When she finished the cigarette, she lay down next to him. Careful not to lean against his bruised body, she closed her eyes and drifted into sleep.

TWENTY-FIVE

Three days after he got back to Chicago, he found the strength to go to the grocery store. He drove himself there and hung his cane on the bar of the shopping cart, then held on to the cart for support. Like an old woman. He bought eggs, bacon, milk and coffee. A loaf of French bread and some cheese. It fit into two plastic bags which he could hold with one hand. He set them on the passenger seat and drove back to his apartment.

There was no elevator; he would have to walk up the stairs unassisted. He made it halfway up the fire escape well before he had to sit down. Go slow, the physician's assistant had said. The body will heal, but if you rush you'll be disappointed and perhaps give up altogether, retreating into pain pills and cable television. So he sat and looked out into the gray alley and parked cars and back windows and listened to the city sounds of weekday traffic and felt the cool air. An existential moment, perfect for a contemplative smoke. But then he couldn't smoke anymore. Fuck.

Thirty-eight years old, he thought. Too

young for self-pity and too old to "go for it." He found he had to concentrate and will himself to hope because if he didn't do that, he might slip into panic. A crippled man who might heal and might not. Frightened of dying and frightened of being weak. Frightened of being like one of those people in the hospital rehabilitation commercials that are supposed to inspire the television audience but usually just horrify them. Frightened of not being able to climb stairs anymore.

There was a car coming down the alley.

It came into view. A dark blue Crown Victoria with the heavy chrome light on the driver's side. A police car.

A woman with dark curly hair and fair skin got out. She locked the car and looked around before resting her eyes on him. Maitland waved to her and she came up the stairs, taking her time. Maitland decided to remain seated until she got to him.

"Hello," she said.

"Hello," Maitland said. "Are you looking for me?"

"Are you Evan Maitland?"

"Yeah."

"Julie Ciskowski." She showed him her police identification. Maitland thought he had seen her before. She said, "I'm a detective. Yes," she said, "I am looking for you."

"Okay."

"I'm here to talk to you about Barry McDermott."

"All right."

"Do you know what happened to him?"

"No."

She waited for him to say something else, but he didn't. She said, "Okay. When was the last time you saw him?"

"In Oklahoma City. In a room with three Jamaicans and, uh, . . . listen, why don't you tell me what you know already. Maybe it would help."

"Hey, I'm just trying to find out."

Maitland smiled to himself. She was a detective and he should have known they could not talk to each other like normal human beings. She wanted him to tell his story, look for the gaps and inconsistencies, then hammer him on it. Well, whatever.

"The last time I saw him he was wearing handcuffs that I put on him. I got shot after that and fell into another room. I shot back, then climbed out the window, ran for a little bit and then passed out. The next thing I remember is waking up in the hospital. So beyond that, I don't know what happened to McDermott. I understand they killed him. But I didn't see it happen."

"Why did they shoot you?"

"To get Barry."

"To get Barry? Was he your property or something?"

"He was my prisoner. They asked me to give him up, I said I wouldn't, then they started shooting."

"I don't understand. Why wouldn't they just shoot you before you got into the house? I mean, what were you doing in the house?"

"Barry asked me to take him there, before we came back home."

"Home — Chicago?"

"Yeah."

"But what did you need to stop at the house for?"

"Because he asked me to take him there."

"For what purpose?"

"I don't know. To pick up his clothes, go to the toilet."

"They have rest stops on the interstate, don't they?"

"Yeah. I suppose they do."

"Why not just take him to the bathroom there?"

"I don't know."

"Did you have a — discussion with these Jamaicans?"

"You mean before the shooting?"

"Yes."

174

"Sort of. They offered me money for Barry. Forty thousand dollars. Said they'd give that to me if I'd just walk away."

"And what was your response?"

Maitland lifted the cane. "Uh . . ."

"You said no."

"Yes. I said no."

"And that was the first time you'd ever met them. In that house."

"Yes."

Maitland was not surprised by the drift of her questions. In fact, he'd been more or less expecting this since he returned to Chicago. He was not really angry with her; he felt comfortable sitting on the fire escape as this woman stood over him and tried to get him to admit that he had made arrangements with the Jamaicans before he got to Oklahoma City. But he had been a cop too, and he was interested in the case beyond the missing lung.

He said, "Can I ask you something?"

Julie said, "Sure."

"Did Terry Specht tell you I was dirty?"

Julie studied him. The man did not seem angry, just curious.

"He spoke with me," she said.

"And he told you I led the posse to Barry, right?"

"Yeah, something like that."

175

"And that I got down there and the deal went bad, and they tried to kill me and I got away. Right?"

"It's along those lines."

"And what evidence do you have to support this theory?"

"Well," Julie said, "it doesn't look good."

"So it smells bad?"

"Yeah, it smells a little."

"Well, the part about the deal going bad, that's true to the degree it went bad for me. My collection fee for bringing Barry back to Cook County would have been thirty thousand dollars. Paid not by the Jamaican posse, but by Charlie Mead, bail bondsman. But I didn't bring him back and I didn't get paid. And now I have one lung and I have to use a cane to go to the grocery store."

"Hey, don't get mad at me."

"I'm not mad at you. Well, no, actually I am a little mad at you. You're accusing me of something pretty vile."

"And you think it's chicken shit?"

"Yeah, I do. I think it's pretty chicken shit."

"Maybe you should have taken the forty."

"Is that what Terry would say?"

"This isn't his case. It's mine."

"You sure about that?"

"Hey —"

"The point is, I didn't take anything from

them." Maitland stood. "It's getting cold," he said. "Would you like some coffee?"

Julie said, "Okay."

They sat at the small oak dining room table. Maitland leaning back his chair, Julie still holding her pen and notebook, consciously avoiding body language that would be interpreted as warm or intimate. He had brewed coffee in a mini–Mr. Coffee maker, a pot holding just enough for three cups of coffee, an indication of a man living comfortably alone.

Maitland told her most everything. His visit to the Admiral gentlemen's club, the interview with Cinnamon Barefoot, the coffeeshop capture of Barry McDermott, the gunfight in Oklahoma City and the hospital room interrogation.

Maitland said, "Are you taping this?" The way he asked, it was clear he would not take offense if she was.

"No."

"You can if you want. Just tell me, though. And send me a copy of the tape afterwards."

"I'm not taping this."

"Do you have tapes of interviews with other witnesses?"

"Yes."

"Can I have copies of those?" He asked even though he knew the answer.

"No."

"Why not?"

"You're not a police officer."

"Am I a suspect? In your investigation, that is?"

"We're just trying to find out what happened."

"Okay." Maitland smiled again. "Well, I'm trying to find out too. How did you hook into this?"

"I was investigating a double homicide on Milwaukee Avenue. Couple of gangbangers shot to death. One victim had four shots to the body, one to the head. Posse signature. Couple of nights later, Cinnamon Barefoot was shot too. You knew about that, didn't you?"

"I found out yesterday."

"Well, that case was not mine. But then you came along, reporting Jamaican posse activity in Oklahoma City. We get e-mails, faxes from the OCPD. Then the M.E.'s office tells us that Cinnamon Barefoot was killed with a 9 millimeter gun, same as the one used on the bangers on Milwaukee Avenue."

"That's a bit attenuated. Nine millimeters are common."

"How about Jamaican posse members chasing a Chicago lawyer down to Oklahoma? Is that common?"

"No."

"That's the connection." Julie said, "You're the connection. You went to see Cinnamon and then they went to see her."

"Well, I'm sorry about that. I'm sorry she died. But doesn't that show something?"

"What do you mean?"

"Doesn't it show that the Jamaicans found out where Barry was from her? Not from me?"

"I don't know."

Maitland sighed and looked at her.

"What is it you came here for?"

"Excuse me?"

"Did you come here to ask me to testify against the Jamaicans? So you can charge them for the murders of Cinnamon Barefoot, Barry McDermott, maybe even attempted murder of me? Or, did you come here to hang something on me?"

"I told you what I came here for."

"No, you really haven't." Maitland stopped. He said, "Were you on television?"

"Pardon?"

"I remember now. You were on the news.

179

Last year. You're the one that shot that guy on the El platform, aren't you?"

"Yes."

"Wow."

Julie Ciskowski was starting to get irritated. Wow. Patronizing her, the arrogant jerk. He would not have said wow if she were a man.

"It was a clean shoot. I was cleared."

Maitland had not meant to patronize her. Though it was indeed probably accurate to say he would not have been wowed had she been a man. He had seen a glimpse of her on television, had read about her in the Tribune and Us magazine. Beyond the media's need to create a hero, he saw an ordinary woman with tremendous courage and imagination. And what amazed him was how ordinary she seemed. A pretty woman with nice skin, a nice girl that probably did well in high school and kept to herself. And going up the steps to the platform had been her idea . . . she was cleared . . . ?

"You were cleared, what do you mean by that?" Maitland said.

"I don't mean anything by it."

"I think you do. I think you mean you were cleared, as opposed to me."

"Okay then. Yes, as opposed to you."

"I see. You think because of what happened years ago, I made a deal with these Jamaicans."

"What would you think?"

"I'd want to know the truth."

"Then we're in agreement."

"Are we?" Maitland said. "Do you want to know the truth, or do you want to build a case against me, show Terry Specht you're smart as well as tough?"

"You're not being fair."

"*I'm* not being fair. Tell me, did you take the time to read the transcript of the arbitration hearing? Cause I got a real feeling you didn't."

"I read the report."

"The internal affairs investigation report."

"Yes."

"Which was written by Terry Specht."

"You keep bringing it back to Terry Specht. He was just the investigator."

"Yes, and he wrote that report."

"He wrote a report, yes. But he did not kill Ronnie Ellis. You did."

"That's right, I did. And I'd do it again tomorrow."

She sighed.

"You see, comments like that don't help you."

"What would you have me say? I'm sorry I

didn't let him kill me first?"

"You could have handled it better."

"Oh, Christ. You cops are all the same."

"You cops — you're a cop."

"I was. Listen, how would you know? How would you know what I should have done? I suppose if you were there, you would have handled it different."

"I'm not saying —"

"Let me speak plainly: I was there. You were not. You don't second-guess the officer who was there. Let me repeat that: you don't second-guess the officer who was there. You cannot do that. You must not do that."

"I've been in the arena too, Maitland."

"I know. And you *weren't* second-guessed. Right? Well, don't go thinking that it had anything to do with your brilliant handling of the Lafayette Station killer. They didn't second-guess you because it was not in their interest to do it. They don't bring internal charges against an officer after the mayor has gone on television and talked about how lucky the city is to have people like her in law enforcement. But go back and switch a few things around. Say, the shooter was black and it turned out he didn't really have a gun, but some shiny object that just happened to look like it was a gun. Is that a clean shoot? Say you're not a detective or patrol officer, but a narcotics agent, working undercover, and you look like a criminal and you take out a guy who's really not that bad a guy, but he's found out what you are and he's going to kill you, so you have to kill him first. Is that a clean shoot? If you testified that you believed it was reasonably believed self-defense and I believed you, I'd say it was. But my take on it would not prevent them from filing criminal charges against you. Not when there's political pressure on the administration to put your ass in the sling. Not for one second. Same woman, same gun. But different circumstances. That's how it works, ma'am. And the sooner you figure that out, the better off you'll be."

"But I didn't do anything wrong."

"Neither did I. Read the hearing transcript, Detective. Don't take my word for it. Don't take Specht's word for it. Don't be so —" He came close to saying, "fucking lazy" but stopped himself, fortunately. "Just read the transcript and draw your own conclusions. Do it for the integrity of your investigation, not for me."

Maitland put his hand to his face and sighed. He remembered where he was and what kind of man he tried to be.

Then he said, "I've got some things I need to do. I'm sorry I spoke to you like that. I was upset. I'm sorry."

"You don't have to apologize," Julie said. She sensed his shame was real. "But I just want to ask one more question."

"All right."

"You won the arbitration and they put you back to work, right?"

"That's right."

"So how come you quit six months later?"

Maitland sighed and thought, what did I just tell you? But she needed an answer. And there were other things. After they reinstated him, they gave him a lot of shit duty and hoot shifts and it was made abundantly clear to him that he would never be allowed to be a detective assigned to robbery-homicide and that at best he could look forward to a career of busting whores on the vice squad. So he quit. And in quitting, acknowledged that — arbitrator or no — the bastards had pretty much beat him in the end. He had more or less landed on his feet after he left. He'd made money selling antiques and from the occasional retrieval of the bond skippers. But bond skipping was buttwork, mostly. Not much thought to it, more talking to the skippers' moms than anything.

Still, he sometimes regretted leaving the department. As a young man, he had signed up with the intention of becoming a detective. Wearing tweed jackets and knit ties and putting murderers behind bars. Using his head. He knew enough about himself to know that he would've been good at it. Better at it than those jackoffs who had leaned on him in Oklahoma City, at least. And he never got there.

You could look back on it and say it was an injustice. But, like the doctor had said, it probably wasn't the right way to look at it. He'd survived, gotten his back pay and stayed out of jail. There was the antique business. And there was Bianca.

He said to the woman who had made detective, "I didn't want to be there."

TWENTY-SIX

Frank Manzoni, manager of Quality Bed and Mattress of Chicagoland, did not push his customers because he did not believe in the hard sale. He gave them mild direction, showed them the merchandise and let them pick out what suited them. He was a big man, a little fat, but wide, tall and imposing. He sat behind the counter on a stool, pointing to the queen-sizes, saying to a pasty guy with a backpack, "David, you go over there, you see what you like. Lay down on 'em, see how they feel. You find something you like, let me know." Frank stayed on his stool and after a moment of hesitation the customer drifted off to the beds. Frank returned to his newspaper.

The store was owned by the Boccaccio family. About half of the inventory was stolen, coming in the front and going out the back. They sold guns there too, some stereo equipment and coats. The guns had once been supplied by the Guzzetti family from the southside, but times had changed. Ed Guzzetti got emphysema and died and Ed Junior was in the penitentiary for con-

186

spiracy to intimidate a witness in a grand jury proceeding. A chickenshit thing to get sent up for, but it had happened and the Boccaccios had turned to another supplier for guns. The new suppliers originated not from Palermo, Sicily, but from West Kingston. Frank was one year over forty, a new generation, and more accepting of change. Business was business.

Frank lifted his gaze from the sports page as a man he knew came toward him.

"Hey, hey," Frank said.

Jukie said, "Hey, mon. How is business?"

"We're getting by, getting by. What do you know?"

"Not much, mon," Jukie said. Then he didn't say anything.

Frank called out to a man named Jimmy to watch the store and he and Jukie walked to the office in the back and shut the door behind them.

Frank said, "What's up?"

Jukie said, "I need you to kill somebody."

"Okay. When?"

"Soon. Today or tomorrow. No later."

Frank said, "You want to pay with guns or money?"

"Whatever you like."

187

TWENTY-SEVEN

Captain Benjamin Cason called Julie Ciskowski into his office and it wasn't until she closed the door behind her that she saw Terry Specht sitting in the corner, hidden from the outside. A bad sign, that. Like he'd wanted to surprise her. Specht was a short, stocky man with glasses and a receding hairline. A little like Barney Rubble, only shitty and mean.

Immediately, Julie wanted to ask her captain, What's *he* doing here? Why didn't you tell me he was going to be here?

But she was a good girl, a team player, a shit eater and she kept quiet.

Captain Cason said, "Julie, Lieutenant Specht asked if he could sit in. You don't mind, do you?"

"No, sir." She looked directly at Cason when she said it, not giving Specht the benefit of a nod.

Cason said, "Tell us what you learned from Maitland."

"Well, sir, I haven't finished my report yet."

"Let's discuss it before you write your report."

That wasn't good, Julie thought. History should be written, then debated. Not the other way around.

"Okay," Julie said, putting noticeable apprehension into it; it did not go unnoticed by Terry Specht, but then she had intended it for him as well as Cason. "Well, he told me what happened in Oklahoma City, why he went down there, what his fee would have been."

"Wait a minute," Specht said. He was holding his hand up for emphasis. "His fee from who?"

"The bonding agency."

"How do you know that?"

"That he was to be paid by Charlie Mead? Charlie Mead confirmed it. It's in his records."

Specht smiled, turned to Cason, asking him to be amused with him over the little girl's naiveté. Julie felt her temper rising.

Specht said, "And you believed him?"

"Are you asking me if I believe Charlie Mead?"

"Yeah."

"Yes, I do believe him. Mead is a businessman, got a reputation as a straight-shooter. Besides, he's got no reason to lie about it."

"Aren't he and Maitland friends?"

"I guess."

"Isn't that reason enough?"

"No, sir, I don't think it is."

Specht smiled again and shook his head. Julie watched it, then turned to Cason and gave him a look that was intended to be meaningful. A look that said, *Why are you allowing this?* She had always been loyal to Cason and she felt she was entitled to some support from him. But Cason did not acknowledge her look. He just said: "What about Maitland?"

"What about him?" Julie said, wondering about Cason now, wondering whose side he was on.

Cason said, "Do you think his story is credible?"

"Well," Julie said. She paused. She was aware of the men in the room and the import of her words and the impact they would have. She felt her heart beating. "Well, I think he is credible, yes."

Specht snorted.

Julie said to her captain, "May I continue?"

Cason said, "Yes."

"To be frank, sir, his story makes sense. He obviously didn't shoot himself. And there's no evidence to support the theory that he had made a deal with the Jamaicans." She saw Specht about to speak, but she looked right at him and continued quickly, "The only evidence, captain, to support that theory is the incident that Maitland was involved in years earlier while he was a police officer. In that matter, as you know, he was alleged by Lieutenant Specht to have killed Ronnie Ellis to cover up his own involvement in drug trafficking activities." Julie stopped, searching for the right words. "I knew, sir, that you would want me to be thorough, so I reviewed the records of that incident, including the transcript of the arbitration hearing and the arbitrator's ruling."

There was a silence in the room, the men waiting for her take on it. She knew that what she said next would be pivotal to them, pivotal to her career. She thought briefly of her husband . . . last night he had said, "Next time, I'll just cook." Like she was hopeless. Not even having the decency to make eye contact when he said it, the pussy. Why did she think of that now?

She said, "Both Maitland, who at that time was a sergeant, and Lieutenant Specht testified at that hearing. The arbitrator wrote that Maitland was a credible witness, that he was honest and forthright and cooperative in the internal investigation. He also wrote that he did not find Lieutenant Specht to be a credible witness and that his report was highly flawed. He wrote that Maitland did not receive a fair investigation."

Cason's body language expressed anger and extreme discomfort. He avoided looking at Terry Specht. And then he did something which Julie never forgave him for.

He said, "And you believe that?" Like she would be a fool if she said yes.

"I believe the arbitrator's ruling is a factor we can't overlook. Sir, it's not really a . . . personal issue. Presuming you wanted to file charges against Maitland, there is no question that the previous matter is going to be relevant. The District Attorney will take issue with it, even if I did not."

Specht said, "What do you mean by that, Detective?"

"Sir?"

"What do you mean, 'even if I did not'? What do you mean by that?"

Oh, shit. She looked to Cason again for some assistance. He didn't give her any, the rotten prick.

"What I mean, Lieutenant, is that I believe Maitland. And I guess I should say for the record that, because of the past incident, I don't believe you should be involved in this investigation."

192

"I'm sorry," Specht said, leaning forward, "what was that?"

"I think your involvement compromises the integrity of the investigation." She felt better after she said it, though she could still feel her heart pounding.

Cason said, "I don't know if you understand what you're saying."

"Actually, I do, sir." Julie paused and said, "Do you understand?"

"You better watch it, Detective. I don't like your tone."

"Christ," Specht said, "she's fallen in love with him."

It took a moment for his words to sink in. It was the twenty-first century and good girl Julie Ciskowski couldn't quite comprehend that a police officer would actually say something like that to her. And not just say it, but say it as if she wasn't even there. It seemed unreal. But then it became real and it so infuriated her that it took a moment to find her bearings.

Julie said, "I . . . what are . . . what is going on here? Lieutenant Specht, would you mind explaining that remark?"

"Julie —" Cason talking now.

"— just what are you implying —"

"— Julie —"

"— I am a police officer —"

"— Jesus Christ —"

"— who are you, *what* are you to be suggesting that I'd —"

"Julie!"

"Do you have the slightest idea of who I am? Of what I've done for this department?"

"Julie, that's enough."

"— Captain — this . . . *person* . . . just accused me of fucking a material witness —"

"He did not. Detective, he did not do that. Now I will not have you making false accusations like that to a superior officer."

Now it had gone from unreal to some freak, parallel universe. The sheer gall of it almost left her speechless. She looked at Captain Cason, realizing how little she knew him. Watching him with his put-on serious face, she felt all sorts of emotions, but the dominating theme word was *coward*. *You miserable, cheap fucking coward.*

She said, "I don't believe this. I really don't believe this." Julie took her glare off Specht and made an effort to speak evenly to her superior, Cason the Betrayer. With effort, she composed herself.

"Sir, let me speak clearly for the record. You are my superior officer and I will obey any lawful order you give me. But if you ask me to prepare a report that I know is false,

194

you will be giving me an order that is unlawful. You will be ordering me to commit
perjury. And subornation of perjury is a
felony in this state."

She stood up.

"If that's all," she said.

Terry Specht said, "You're going to
regret this."

Julie didn't answer right away. She
stopped at the door and gave Specht a slow,
appraising look.

"I doubt it," said the hero of Lafayette
Station.

She walked out, closing the door behind
her.

TWENTY-EIGHT

Two men in a dark green '93 Lexus LS400. Behind the wheel Nick Vasto, next to him Frank Manzoni. They both wore dark stocking caps. There was an Ithaca pump shotgun on the floorboard of the passenger side, Frank's hand on the stock. They had the windows cracked and there was a Fleetwood Mac song on the radio. "Don't Stop Thinking About Tomorrow." Frank remembered hearing it a lot when Clinton first ran for president. Yesterday's gone.

They were parked across the street from the antique store. They saw the good-looking, exotic woman wearing a skirt and a sweater leave the store, get into a Mercedes-Benz E420 and drive away. The lights to the store went off and the large display window became dark, reflecting the man's black BMW parked in front.

Nick Vasto said, "We can go in now, do it that way. He's probably alone."

Frank, the professional, shook his head. "We stick with the plan."

A few minutes later, they saw the front door open and the man walk out and shut it behind him, then locking it.

Frank said, "Get ready."

Nick started the car. Frank picked up the shotgun, already racked and ready as Nick timed it, edging slowly toward the BMW as Maitland came around to the driver's side and got in, his cane pulled in before the door closed.

It was the cane that drew Nick Vasto's attention. The man didn't look old; it was unusual for him to have a cane. It made him feel uneasy and he didn't know why.

"Go," Frank said.

The Lexus pulled up even with the BMW. Frank leaned out the window and pointed the shotgun toward the driver. Maitland became aware of the car next to him, the big man in the stocking cap, the gun, and fell to his right as the window exploded with the blast. Fragments of glass blew into the car and Maitland heard that awful racking sound that puts another slug in the chamber as he sucked in his stomach and moved the gearshift into reverse and stomped on the accelerator. He heard another shotgun blast and then felt a jolt as the BMW knocked a motorcycle over that had been parked behind him.

He sat up and saw the reverse lights of the Lexus, backing toward him, and he shifted into drive and passed them going forward as they passed him going backward and he hammered it toward the next intersection, lifting his foot off the accelerator to make the left turn, then pressing it back down.

Christ God, there was too much traffic, people going home from work and blocking up intersections and taking their goddam time doing it and the dark Lexus loomed in his rearview mirror, dodging in and out of cars that were moving too slow and Maitland was stuck behind two SUV's that seemed to be conversing with each other at twenty-five mph so he whipped it out into the oncoming lane and saw a Lincoln buck up and chatter as its driver stood on the brakes and Maitland brought the 750 ship back in front of the SUV's and heard a cacophony of angry horns and screeching tires.

He kept going.

He remembered that he had started keeping a gun in his glove compartment since his return from the hospital. His Glock .45, loaded but not racked and he had locked the fucking glove compartment for some reason and it would be too much time, would take too much time, too *too* much time to stop the car and shut it off so he could use the key to unlock the glove compartment and pull the gun out and pull back the slide as the men in the Lexus caught up to him and blew his brains out.

He was up to eighty now on a four-way city street that was not cut out for this sort of driving. He needed both hands on the wheel because if he wasn't concentrating he would end up piling into another car and killing himself and others and Jesus, he needed time, time to think it out, time to stay alive and think about how to escape his executioners who seemed very determined. Seemed professional.

He saw cars up ahead bunched up, waiting for the light to change and thought, if I stop I die, so he went around, in the oncoming lane which was empty now but wouldn't be for long so he laid on the horn and hoped that no one would come around the intersection making a left or right turn and someone did, a Ford Taurus, and Maitland brought the BMW into the narrow gap between the Ford on his left and the line of sitting cars and pushed it through and heard a horrible screech as the rear of his car scraped past some part of the Ford though he didn't wait around to see how bad it was as he shot into the intersection and heaved right and headed up the road.

The light turned green and the cars

moved forward slowly but finally gave Nick Vasto the opening he needed as he turned right and floored it, the powerful Lexus reaching seventy, then eighty very soon and they saw the tail end of the BMW hurtling away before them, but he didn't have an open road and they started to close the distance.

The driver's side window of the BMW was gone and cold air pelted Maitland in the face, bringing an involuntary tear to his eye. He was thinking about his CLEET training when he first became a police officer and how the instructor had taught them that an officer's car can become his coffin when someone wanted to shoot him. That's why they had taught them to remove the seatbelts before they arrived on a shots-fired call. You don't want to be strapped in that seat when they're wanting to shoot you.

Clear the car.

But how? Where?

Pull over and stop, then get out and run.

Run where? How far with this cane? Yeah, guy . . . hobble along as the men in wool caps snicker at the sight of the poor cripple taking a load of buckshot in the back.

A man and a woman riding their bicycles in the bitter cold heard the BMW coming fast toward them, the horn blaring intermittently, and they slowed and stopped. Watched the BMW blur by, going about ninety. Stood still as the Lexus shot by seconds later.

Maitland saw the red and blue sign indicating the interstate and thought, there. He slowed the car, a bit, just enough to be able to make the left turn onto the entrance ramp without losing control, then pressed the accelerator onto the floor. He alternated his concentration between slipping into westbound traffic and the rearview mirror. He soon saw the Lexus coming down the ramp after him.

Okay, he thought.

Okay.

He felt it then, didn't really think about it, but knew in his gut what he was going to do . . . it was a hard, primal thing. A matter of survival, not a thing to think about.

The Lexus was coming after him, closing distance again. Maitland got his cell phone out of his jacket pocket and dialed 911. The dispatcher came on.

Maitland said, "I'm driving northbound on the interstate. There are a couple of guys chasing me in a green Lexus LS400. They're trying to kill me. I'm in a 1990 black BMW 750iL."

"Where are you? What's the last exit

number you passed?"

"I don't know. Please hurry."

He clicked off the phone. He eased off the accelerator. Slightly, but enough. He moved the car into the center lane, watched the side mirror as the Lexus drew closer and closer. He waited until they were about one car length behind and he lifted his foot completely off the accelerator and touched the brake. The Lexus moved past him, slowed, and Maitland hit the accelerator and swung the wheel left.

He saw the look of surprise on the shooter's face just before the tank-like BMW rammed into the passenger's door. Maitland swung the car out then back again. This time he punched the Lexus up against the concrete divider. He heard the men shouting and eased off as Nick Vasto floored the Lexus ahead and over to the center lane. Maitland shifted into the left passing lane, and, knowing how hard it was to drive and shoot at this speed, let the driver of the Lexus get ahead just a little bit before speeding up next to him. Nick Vasto looked at him just before Maitland smashed the BMW into the driver's side, pulled out, then swung it back in and rammed him again.

The Lexus swerved over to the right, where

Maitland wanted it, and Frank Manzoni turned just in time to see the horrifying sight of the grey side of an eighteen-wheel truck coming closer, closer, then making contact as the Lexus was forced into it.

Metal against metal, screeches, sparks. The car's side and roof crumpling.

Frank shifted over, almost into Nick Vasto's lap.

"He's a fucking madman," Nick said. "A fucking madman."

Frank Manzoni threw the shotgun in the back seat then climbed over as Nick pulled the Lexus clear of the semi and went into the right lane. Frank didn't even get a chance to roll the window down when he saw the BMW veer toward them again.

It hit the Lexus hard and held on, shoving it now, off the road and onto the shoulder, then off the shoulder as it pulled away and they sailed off into space.

The Lexus was going about ninety when it went airborne, flew about a hundred feet before it came down on green grass with hard ground beneath, the front biting in before it flipped end over end, twisting and bouncing off the earth before coming to a rest.

The car did not explode into flames as it often does in the movies. It didn't make any difference; the men inside died anyway.

TWENTY-NINE

The Illinois Highway Patrol officer asked him why he had to run them off the road. Maitland said he didn't mean to, but they were shooting at him and had they seen the blown-out driver's side window of his car? The patrolman told him he should have called the police, let them handle it. Maitland said, "I did. You guys didn't show up until it was over."

The patrolman sighed before turning to another traffic cop and saying, "Looks like self-defense."

Yeah, but there were two dead men in the ambulance now. Traffic was slowed to two lanes, creeping by three highway patrol cruisers and a car from Skokie Police, a couple of fire engines. Flares and orange cones glowing in the dark. Getting colder now.

The other patrolman said, "Yeah, but you could have driven to a rest stop or something." Like it would have helped.

Maitland said, "Listen, I've given you a statement."

"Did you know these guys?"

"I already told you I didn't."

"Yeah?"

"I told him."

"I don't know about that. Why would they come after you if they didn't know you?"

"Why don't you ask them?"

"I can't ask them. They're dead."

"Well, then you don't get answers and my car got totaled. I guess we both got hosed."

They let him go, the second cop saying, "Watch it" or something to that effect, the dumbshit, and Maitland got out of there before he lost his temper and smacked his cane across the punk's ugly face. Fucking highway cop, wanting to yell at somebody and putting it on Maitland because he was there to put it on. He kept both hands on the wheel as he drove back into town to keep them from shaking.

He parked the ruined car in the garage, went into his apartment and poured a double whiskey. He sat in his leather chair with the .45 on the table next to him, ready to shoot anyone who tried to come through the door.

Christ. Two weeks ago, he had two lungs and a nice used high-performance car. Men weren't trying to kill him. Two weeks ago, he had a life he could live with.

The telephone rang.

"Yeah."

"Mr. Maitland?"

"Yeah."

"Detective Ciskowski. I just heard about what happened."

"Yeah?"

"Are you all right?"

"I'm fine."

"What happened?"

"A couple of guys in a Lexus tried to kill me. They had a shotgun."

"You know who they were?"

"The state patrol told me their names. Frank Manzoni and Nick Vasto. You know them?"

"Yeah, I ran a check. Vasto has no record. Frank Manzoni is dirty though. Been arrested twice. A mobster."

"They do business with Jamaicans?"

"Maybe."

Maitland reclined back in his chair. "Well," he said, "that's something. Can you make the connection, maybe arrest these guys so I can live past next week?"

"I don't know, Evan."

"What's the problem?"

"Well, here's what we have: Barry McDermott represented Richard Lawes, a known associate of Trevor Collins. Trevor

Collins is the leader of the Raetown Posse. Heard of them?"

"No."

"They're into a lot of bad, bad things. Guns, drugs, etcetera."

"What did Barry represent Richard on?"

"Possession of an unregistered firearm. But it was found on a bad search and McDermott got it dismissed."

"The man I saw —" Maitland stopped. "Barry called him by his name. Peter."

"Peter. Peter what?"

"I don't know. He just said Peter. There were two other men there. Maybe one of them was Richard Lawes. Where is he now?"

"I don't know."

"Maybe I killed him."

"Why do you think that?"

"I shot someone through the door. If he's got a gunshot wound or he's missing, that will place him at that house in Oklahoma City."

"Okay."

"Can you check it out?"

"Sure."

Sure, Julie thought, if I'm not pulled off the investigation. If I weren't working for assholes who are more concerned about their little dick egos and forming alliances against women cops. Sure.

207

THIRTY

He took the train to work the next morning and found he could walk half the distance from the stop to the antique store without the cane. Not steady comfortable walking, but getting there. He bought a coffee in a to-go cup then opened up the shop. He drank half the coffee before grabbing a broom and sweeping up the broken glass in the street in front of the shop.

Bianca saw him with the broom when she got to work.

"What's up?" she said, taking in this unusual sight.

Maitland regarded her fresh morning beauty before answering. Seeing her in a different way now, though at the same time seeing her as he had always seen her. He remembered seeing her in the morning at a low-budget hotel room in Missouri, cleaned, bright and beautiful. He remembered waking in the night to find her lying next to him, curled, her back to him. He had wanted to touch her then, reach out and put his hand on her back, slip it around her waist and go back to sleep. But he was nauseous with medication and pain and he wondered halfway if he was hallucinating the whole thing. So he remained on his back till sleep came back to him. When he woke the next morning, she was coming back in the door of the hotel room with a cup of coffee and a donut. For him. And he had to watch it then, because the medication was liable to make him spoil it all by saying somethin' stupid, telling her he loved her. So he was careful and just said, "Thank you."

He thought of how he looked now with the broom in his hand and, for some reason, thought of that sweet, simple-minded kid in *The Last Picture Show* who made a habit of sweeping the middle of the street. He eventually gets run over by a truck and some brute asks just what the hell was he doing out here and Timothy Bottoms cries out in anguish, "He was sweeping, you sons a bitches!"

He could let Bianca think he was simple-minded.

But, then, he really couldn't.

"Just sweeping," he said.

"Someone break something?"

"Uh, yeah. Listen, I need to talk to you."

He told her all of it. About the man he had

killed years earlier, about the man he had probably killed in Oklahoma City, about the men he had killed yesterday. He waited for her to say something. Something like, "But this can't be who you are." Or, "But you don't seem like a violent man." Something comforting and nice.

It didn't happen. She looked at him, almost angry, and said, "Why are you telling me this?"

It was a tone he didn't like and he wondered if he knew what was behind it. Then he wondered if he wondered. He said, "What do you mean?"

"Why are you telling me this?" She said it slower this time, like he hadn't been listening or he was simple-minded.

Maitland waited, searching for the words.

"I'm telling you because — because I don't think it's safe to work with me."

"You want to split up the partnership?"

"Yes."

"Why?"

"I just told you why. I was parked out front last night, about five minutes after you left, and guys drove up and pointed a shotgun out the window and blew out the window of my car. Maybe they'll send different guys out here tomorrow. Fuck, I don't know. What are we supposed to do, close the store?"

"I told you not to go."

"No, you didn't."

"Yes, when you called me from your car."

"No, you did not tell me not to go. You didn't tell me not to go. You just got mad at me because I left without asking your permission."

"Yeah, and look what it led to."

"I'm not sure I believe this. You think I wanted this to happen?"

"On some level, I do."

"You're crazy."

"Evan, you've got a good business here. You make a good living, and I think you like it. Why, *why*, would you go down to Oklahoma to chase a fugitive? What's wrong with you? What's missing from your life that you have to chase people? That you have to have guns in your car, in your home . . . that you. . . ."

"Bianca, if I didn't have the gun, I'd be dead now."

"Oh, Christ, you are not even listening to me. It's not about the gun, Evan. It is not about the — gun. It's about you. You did not have to go down there. You did not have to do that. And now look what you've done. You bring this — you bring this here."

"I know I did. I'm sorry."

After a moment she said, "Sorry isn't going to take care of it."

She walked out of his office.

THIRTY-ONE

Natalie brought in a plate of jerk chicken and handed it to Trevor Jim. She said hello to Jukie. Jukie said hello back and she left them alone.

Trevor Jim kept his focus on the soccer match on television. Manchester United vs. Chelsea. Trevor Jim was a Chelsea fan; he remembered growing up with a black-and-white photo of Georgie Best in his room.

Without turning his gaze from the screen, Trevor said, "Can they trace Frank back to you?"

"No."

"You sure?"

"Yeah, mon. I'm sure."

Trevor turned to look at him. Appraising him, then shaking his head.

Jukie said, "Trevor, you not gonna blame me for that. You the one told me to ask Frank."

"Maybe you should have gone with them."

"What good would that have done?"

Trevor looked at him again. "I don't know, actually," he said.

Briefly, Jukie thought of shooting Trevor Jim in the face. He could do it that simple, then kill the man's woman and leave. He had about forty thousand in cash in his apartment. He could take it and leave town, maybe fly back to Kingston. Maybe move to Florida.

Jukie said, "You want to talk trash fuckery to me, go ahead. But you the one givin' the orders, mon."

Trevor shrugged. "But you the one let him get away in the first place. An' he saw you. Maybe he tell police about you, point to your picture in a file, an' it come back to me." Trevor said, "You see where I'm going? If you do, then you know I'm not so bad a fellah as you think."

Jukie saw it. Trevor was telling him if he wanted him dead, he'd be dead. Maybe it'd be Maurice that would come after him. Maybe even Trevor Jim himself. There would not be much he could do to stop it, outside of leaving town. That, or flipping on Trevor to the police. And that would mean prison time for him.

Trevor said, "I'm giving you a chance to clean it up. You see?"

"Yeah, I see."

"Maurice and I been talking. We think maybe Barry left the money with the girl down in Oklahoma City. We going down there tomorrow pay her a visit. You stay here. Take care of Mr. Maitland."

THIRTY-TWO

Terry Specht came into the store that afternoon. Bianca didn't know him, but she didn't like his look, his mean smile or his attitude. She said, "Can I help you?"

He took out his police identification and shoved it towards her. He said, "I need to see your boss."

"I am the boss, here. Did you want to see Evan?"

"Yeah. Why don't you get him." Giving her an order.

"Sir, you are in my store. You don't talk to me like that."

"It's all right, Bianca." Evan stood behind her, having come out of the back room.

She left and Maitland stood before the Terry Specht he remembered. Fatter now, but still the same bureaucrat bully who liked to thrust his badge at people who'd piss on him at a cocktail party and other people who wouldn't shiv him in the guts. He didn't handle power well, the kind of man who had no business being in law enforcement but often is.

In a tired voice, Maitland said, "What

216

do you want, Terry?"

Terry looked around the store, performing, pretending to take in the fancy-schmancy merchandise.

"Selling furniture now, huh?"

"Yeah. Selling furniture. What is it I can do for you?"

"I'd like to talk to you about your little road rage incident yesterday."

"That was in Skokie. A little out of your jurisdiction."

"Knocked off a couple of mobsters, crewmen for the Boccaccio family. What is it about you and the people you associate with?"

"Self-defense, Terry."

"Not what I heard."

"Who'd you hear it from?"

Terry didn't answer. Not right away, anyway, so Maitland picked it up.

"Yeah, that's what I thought. Another bluff. God, Terry, you haven't changed at all. You know what your problem is?"

"Why don't you tell me?"

"You're lazy. You come up with your theories, but you never put a case together. It's witnesses, evidence that will hold up in court. *That's* how you build a case. You, you just want to get by with shadows and fog. Insinuations. You taping this conversation?"

"No."

"Yeah, you are. Ah, fuck it. I don't care. What do you want? Do you want me to tell you if I knew those guys? What they were doing coming after me? Well, as I told Detective Ciskowski, they were probably hired by the same people that tried to kill me in Oklahoma City. That should be pretty apparent to a detective."

"How much did they pay you?"

"How much did who pay me?'

"The Jamaicans. How much did they pay you to take them to Barry McDermott?"

"Oh, another theory. They didn't pay me anything, Terry. Nobody paid me anything to find Barry McDermott. I found him because the bail bondsman offered me the standard fee to find him and bring him back. You got any evidence that says otherwise, forward it to the District Attorney."

"You're dirty."

"Yeah, whatever. Listen, I'm not a cop anymore. I'm just a citizen. So, I'm going to invoke Fifth Amendment now and refuse to answer any more of your questions. That said, Mrs. Lincoln, you see anything you want to buy?"

"You're dirty and you're going down."

"I guess you don't. Well, if I can't interest you in any of our wares, you should probably get back to work, hotshot."

"You're going to jail, jagoff."

"Right, spanky. Have a nice day."

Maitland almost smiled as he watched Specht just raise his hand, then lower it — the pussy — then storm out of the shop. Terry wouldn't dare try to hit Maitland. He wasn't that sort of cop and never had been.

He felt a touch on his arm and turned to see Bianca. Touching him reassuringly, like a wife. Touching him in a way he needed.

She said, "Man, you pretty tough guy when you want to be."

"Selling antiques is a tough business."

"Why did you call him Mrs. Lincoln?"

"That's an American . . . joke." He turned to her, persuaded himself not to kiss her. "I'll explain it to you sometime."

She said, "I don't think he got it either."

THIRTY-THREE

The train rattled by on the elevated rail, diverting the attention of the drivers for a brief moment as it passed over a midtown street, lit up, silvery; then it was gone and hurtling farther into the city.

Maitland stood on the train, holding onto the pole. He was getting stronger and at times he would take weight off the pole and put all of it on his legs. He stood and he thought of the events of his day.

It was good to be able to stand. His wounds were healing, but he'd feel better once he bought another car. He knew that it would be nice to be able to tell people that having his car totaled was the best thing that ever happened to him because it made him realize how much simpler life was when you relied on public transportation. Nice if he believed it. But he didn't. He wanted to be driving a car. He did not want to ride trains.

The insurance adjustor had called Maitland at work after he'd finished examining the car. He'd given Maitland heat about it too, saying he didn't know if a claim could be made if there was intentional conduct. Maitland said he'd paid extra money for collision and comprehensive coverage and if the guy was going to be tough about it, he'd call a lawyer and ask him to look into a bad faith suit against the insurance company. The adjustor asked him how he knew about bad faith, was he a lawyer himself or something, and Maitland told him he'd read about a multimillion-dollar verdict in the newspaper on a case where an old lady's insurance company had treated her wrong and he was beginning to understand now why the jury hammered them. The adjustor said he didn't want to argue about it and that the claim would "probably" be paid, and Maitland said it better be and got off the phone. He wondered about it afterwards, wondered if he even knew what he was talking about. Then he decided it didn't matter then and he would worry about it later if the insurance company actually did try to stiff him.

He said, "Jesus Christ" too loud after hanging up the phone and Bianca looked at him but did not ask him what was the matter because it was only an hour or so after they had argued — about what he didn't understand — and she still didn't want to talk to him. The bad feelings and the anger drifted away after Terry Specht came in though and she came and stood by his side and he had wanted to kiss her and ask her to come home with him and stay the night in his bed and they could talk about what it meant in the morning, but he didn't because that would be adultery, which was bad enough, but adultery with someone you love is about a dozen times more complicated. So he behaved himself and thought more seriously about getting out of the partnership with her.

What had happened? He had known her for three years and never really felt like this. They liked and respected each other and kept their boundaries. He knew her husband; Max was his name. He was a tall, slim grey-haired guy who drove a modest Toyota Solara and looked kind of like Richard Gere only a little more effeminate. He was Bianca's second husband and he had a grown daughter from his first marriage. Max managed a restaurant in the Marshall Fields department store. He was a nice guy. Not the sort of man Maitland could get drunk and joke with or relate to, but an all-right guy.

If there was something that could justify taking his woman away . . . Bianca talking about his drug habit or gambling sickness or Bianca coming in with a black eye . . . something that would justify persuading her to leave him . . . oh, shit, that was insane. Hoping that

Bianca would come in the store with a black eye? What a shameful, cruel thought. He might just as well hope Max would get run over by a bus. In the name of true love, no less. You're losing it, Evan. Losing your fucking mind.

The train came to his stop and he got off and walked down the steps using the rail. He walked to the steps of his apartment and started up them without first stopping for a rest. Progress, my boy.

He let himself in and saw that there was a message on his answering machine.

"Mr. Maitland, this is Detective Ciskowski. Would you call me?" She left her cell number.

He called her.

She said, "Where are you?"

"I'm at home. Where you called me."

"Oh. Listen, I'd like to talk to you."

"Okay."

"Can we meet someplace?"

"Well, I just got home and I don't have a car. . . ."

"Would you mind if I came over?"

"No."

"Good. I'll be there in about fifteen minutes."

Maitland hid his sigh. He was tired and moody, but she was about the only law enforcement officer he seemed to have on his side anymore and he didn't want to offend her.

"Okay."

There was a pause and Maitland thought she had clicked off the phone. But then heard her voice again.

"Evan?"

Using his first name, she sounded uncertain.

Maitland said, "Yeah?"

"I was pulled off the case today."

THIRTY-FOUR

The summary sheet listed the following:

Peter Blake — BM, DOB: 8 Aug 1970, AKA Jukie Blake ARRESTED 29 MAY 1999 BY CHICAGO POLICE DEPARTMENT ON CHARGES OF OBSTRUCTING/RESISTING ARREST, POSSESSION W/ INTENT TO DISTRIBUTE

Maitland said, "That's it?"

Julie said, "That's his only arrest. His file jacket says he is known to be associated with the Raetown Posse. The same one I told you about earlier." She pointed. "There's a photo."

Maitland studied it. A smiling man with a becoming goatee.

"That's him," he said.

Julie sat back in her chair. The cup of coffee sat on the table in front of her where Maitland had put it.

He said, "What?"

"You'd testify to that in court?"

"Of course I would."

"Then you know what's going to happen."

"Yeah. The defense lawyer will bring up my past. So what? I've testified about it before."

"Suppose the DA files charges, Blake will say he acted in self-defense. I can see it happening."

Maitland regarded her.

He said, "Are you speaking someone else's thoughts? Because it sounds like you are."

"Look, I'm not here on behalf of Terry Specht or Captain Cason. I came here to help you."

"Captain Cason, you mean Ben Cason?"

"Yes. He's my captain."

"What does he have to do with it?"

"He's the one that pulled me off the case."

Maitland stared at her, the reality starting to set in.

"Do you mean to tell me they're not going to recommend charges be filed?"

"I think so," she said, looking away from him when she said it.

"Jesus."

"You know where I stand."

"No, I don't think I do."

Julie almost scowled at him.

"Well, I got pulled off the case. I would think that would give you some indication."

"Don't get mad at me. It's not you they're trying to kill."

"Why are you talking to me like that? I didn't have to come here."

"You didn't . . . ? — you're a police officer. You're supposed to protect me from people like this."

"People like who?"

"People like Jukie Blake and Trevor Collins. And, when push comes to shove, people like Terry Specht."

"What do you want me to do? Terry Specht is a lieutenant. Cason's my captain. What do you want me to do?"

"Don't you see what's going on? They're not pulling you off the case because they think I'm not in danger. They're pulling you off because they know I am."

She looked at him for a moment and then found that she couldn't quite look at him anymore. When she looked at him again he knew she agreed.

Maitland said, "Jesus, you know?"

"What do you want me to do?"

"Arrest the motherfucker."

"It's not my case anymore. I can't arrest him."

"Why did you come here?"

"I came here to — "

"To what?"

"I came here to. . . ." She looked at him again. She was a good and honest cop and she was ashamed.

"You came here to warn me."

"Yeah."

"Is that it?"

"Yeah."

Maitland stared at her, furious. Though not at her. Well, maybe at her. "Jesus," he said, disgusted. He stood up and walked away.

He was looking out the window, his back to her, when he heard her speak.

"I don't know if you understand," she said. "What it is . . . what it's like to be a woman. A woman cop. I was never . . . like that, you know. Never what you would call a hardcore feminist. I don't think I even liked feminists. I was a tomboy, a tough girl. But I liked being a girl. And I liked men. And I liked being a cop. I used to, anyway. And now I just feel like a stranger."

She remained at the table, sitting in her chair and looking down at the floor.

She said, "You remember that woman that used to be the department spokesperson? The one you see on television. The dyke? I never met her. She's probably an okay person. But she couldn't do what I could do. She's a bureaucrat, an admin person. See, that's what they want the women to be. Administrative. PR. Personnel. Shit, girl's stuff. But if you do their job as well as they do, then . . . they resent you."

Maitland, the marked man, said, "You're telling me your problems." He did not turn to address her.

"Yeah," she said. "I don't really have anyone else to talk to. I don't really have any friends anymore. All the people I know are cops. You know how tribal they are; you join the force and two years later you can't really relate to any civilians. They don't trust you or, at a minimum, they don't really feel comfortable with you. John, my partner . . . he's okay. But he doesn't really understand me. If I talked to him, confided in him . . . he'd misunderstand it. Take it as a weakness. Poor little lady."

"Poor little lady."

Julie seemed not to hear him.

She said, "Do you know how it felt when I killed that man?"

Maitland turned to look at her. "I might."

"I won't say it felt good, exactly. Not that. But it felt necessary. And I felt I had *done*

something good. Do you see the difference?"

"Yeah."

"I mean I didn't feel ashamed. Shaken,
but not . . . ashamed."

"You feel any shame now?" Maitland
said. He was still angry.

"Yes."

He regarded her. She really was a beautiful woman.

Maitland said, "Well, that's something."

"Can I have some more coffee?"

"Help yourself."

She did.

Then she started to speak again, like she
had to.

"It's good coffee."

"Thank you."

"You don't mind my staying?"

"No. I just need to — no, I don't mind."

"We need to talk about this," she said.
"We need to talk about what you're going to
do."

"Why?"

"Because you're in trouble."

"I'm glad you see it." Maitland changed
his expression. "No, I am. Really."

"Yeah?"

"Yeah."

Moments passed. Julie took a look at

Maitland's apartment, the walls and the furnishings and the kitchenware. They said something about him.

She said, "I think I should tell you something else."

"What?"

"Lieutenant Specht accused me of fucking you."

Maitland snorted.

"What?"

"He did."

"Jesus, what a piece of shit."

"He is a piece of shit. But the real trash is Ben. Ben sided with him."

"Ben believes that too?"

"You know, I don't know. That's what makes me so sick about it. I'm not even sure Ben believes it, but he's going to side with Specht anyway. It's just so disgusting."

"I'm sorry, Julie."

"I've just never felt so betrayed by someone. I've never felt this betrayed. Ever. Not even by my husband."

Maitland said, "Your husband — I don't understand."

"Oh. Well, I think my husband's having an affair," she said.

Maitland felt a thud in his heart. A guilty mind. He said, "Why do you think that?"

"Women always figure that shit out. If

they want to, anyway. It might be someone he met through his job. Sometimes he comes home late, I've smelled perfume on him . . . it's easy to figure out." She said it like she wished it were difficult.

Maitland said, "Have you talked to him about it?"

"No. No. I'm not sure I care, really. It's humiliating, I guess, but I'm really not sure I care. It was getting pretty stale before — he's not a cop — and then after the shooting at Lafayette Station, that was it."

"What did that do?"

She smiled at him from across the room. "I'm surprised you have to ask that," she said.

"I don't get it."

"See . . . men aren't comfortable with warrior women."

"You see yourself as a warrior?"

"No. I don't see myself that way. Not at all. But he's . . . he's got issues with it. Some primal . . . man thing. Dan's never really challenged me before; I mean, he's never been the sort to start arguments. But now he does. He looks for reasons to best me. Reasons to hurt me. There was this friend of mine from college; Dan even knew her. She and her boyfriend — his name was Mark something — they were both pre-med. They both took the same classes. Both applied to medical school. Anyway, I think you can see where this is going. She got accepted and he, he did not. He didn't get accepted anywhere. And do you know what those dumbshits did?"

"They got married."

"Yeah. God, we used to have dinner with them, Dan and I. And I used to *like* Mark. I thought he was an okay guy. But the way he'd treat her. Telling her she didn't know how to order wine, rolling his eyes when she pronounced a country wrong. Just a complete asshole. Jesus, I'm surprised she stayed with him."

"She stayed with him?"

She shrugged. "I guess. We lost touch. Anyway, after the shooting I realized that my husband had become Mark."

"I'm sorry."

"It's not your fault. Anyway, I can't stay with him." She looked directly at Maitland, "What is wrong with men, anyway?"

"We're pussies."

She smiled at him, and then seemed to appraise him.

"Were you ever married?"

"Yeah."

"Divorced?"

"Yeah."

"What happened?"

Maitland shrugged. "Married young, grew apart. That's pretty much it."

"Did you have children?"

"No. You?"

"No. I wanted to, but — no. I'd like to sometime. Not with him, though. Maybe I'll quit."

"Quit what? The department or the marriage?"

"Both."

Maitland took another look at her. The coal black hair and ruddy face and bright, intelligent eyes. She was all right.

He said, "You can't quit now."

She looked at him, confused.

"Why not?" she said.

"Because I need you to stay."

THIRTY-FIVE

Sergeant Jeff Johnson screamed but the red cotton shirt that was wrapped around his mouth kept any sound from coming out. It felt like his thigh was burning and he looked down to see the red licorice strip of blood forming on his leg.

Trevor said, "Calm down, soldier. I didn't cut no artery. I can, though."

Jeff Johnson was in his skivvies; white shirt and shorts, sitting on a kitchen chair with his hands and arms bound. His ankles were tied to the legs of the chair. He wanted to think this wasn't real. But his leg was searing with pain and the blood was flowing.

Trevor wiped the knife off on a piece of cloth.

Trevor said, "We gon' to take the shirt out of your mouth." He gestured to Maurice, leveling a sawed-off shotgun at his face. "You scream, we gon' give you somethin' to scream about. Nod if you understand."

Jeff Johnson nodded.

Trevor untied the shirt and Jeff Johnson

gasped for air, sobbing.

Trevor said, "Where did the woman go?"

Jeff said, "She left me. I swear to God, she did. There is no money in this house . . . don't you see . . . that's why she left. She left here because she found the money. I don't have it. I didn't get back here until two days ago. I swear! Look on the kitchen table. Look! It's my orders. They're dated. I swear to you, she was gone by the time I got back."

Trevor gestured to Maurice and Maurice went to the kitchen.

Jeff Johnson reflected on the gross ironies of life. A year and a half overseas, working mostly in logistics and support development. He knew soldiers that had been captured and even a couple that had been killed. But he had made it home to his loving wife that had left him and then a couple of island moolies had broken in his house, surprising him and knocking him unconscious. He woke up alive, but with his pants pulled off and tied to this chair. More frightened than he'd ever been in his life. These guys were cool and methodical. Like they had been trained by a Brazilian torture squad.

Maurice came back with some papers. Trevor removed a pair of glasses from his breast pocket and read them over. "Huh," he said.

Trevor said, "Okay. Where you think she went?"

"I think she went back to Chicago. She hated it here."

"That's the problem when you marry these out-of-town girls," Trevor said. "Sooner or later they want to go home."

Johnson said, "I hope you find her. She's a whore."

Maurice said, "Hey."

His tone was quiet and it chilled Jeff to the bone.

And Maurice said, "That's not a nice thing to say about your wife." He seemed serious when he said it. Offended. Jeff Johnson managed to control his bladder. He wasn't sure which one of them scared him more.

Trevor said, "When you going back to the war?"

"The war's over."

"When you going back to the Army?"

"Next week."

Trevor Jim put the point of the knife close to Jeff Johnson's eye.

"All right, soldier bwoy," he said. "We going to let you live. But if you call the police on us, anything like that, we gon' come back here and cut your eye out. You understand?"

They left him tied to the chair.

Walking to the car, Maurice said, "He probably bleed to death anyway."

Trevor said, "He got time to get himself out of those ropes. He a soldier, isn't he?"

THIRTY-SIX

Julie said, "You need me? What do you mean you need me?"

Maitland said, "I need you to stay at the department. I'll need your help."

Julie frowned. "My help. I don't like the sound of that."

"I'm not going to ask you to do anything dishonest."

"I don't know. I told you, I'm off the case."

"And you came here."

"So what?"

Maitland thought about crossing the room to stand close to her, but decided not to.

"Why?" he asked.

"I told you. To warn you."

"Okay," Maitland said. "You've warned me. Now you know without police protection these men are going to kill me. Your people have sentenced me to death."

"Ah, they . . ." She wanted to defend the department, but was having trouble doing it.

"It's the same thing," Maitland said, cutting her thoughts off. "Listen, I can't live like this. I can't stay awake all night waiting for someone to break into my apartment with a shotgun. I can't carry a sidearm at my place of business. I can't subject people I care about to — I can't go on like this."

She looked at him then in a way that made him uncomfortable.

She said, "Who do you care about?"

He sighed. It wouldn't be proper to discuss it with her.

"That's my business."

"Do you have a girlfriend?"

"No."

"When's the last time you —"

"It's been a while."

"What about me?"

There was a silence between them then as they looked at each other and contemplated the moment. Maitland had never been much of a ladies' man and he didn't believe any man that claimed to understand women. Still, he knew something of human nature. He sensed Julie Ciskowski was not a player in this arena, just a flesh and blood woman.

He said, "You've never been unfaithful to your husband, have you?"

"No."

"Why start now?"

"My marriage is over."

"Are you sure?"

"Yes."

"I'm not so sure you're sure."

"Don't tell me what I'm sure of," she said. "Besides, what concern is it to you? We could be together. For the night. I wouldn't ask anything of you afterwards."

"How do you know I wouldn't ask something of you?"

She smiled. "You're so full of shit," she said. "Men don't ask for anything after. They take what they can get. You're no different."

"No," Maitland said, "probably not." But he was thinking again of a sparse hotel room in Missouri . . . the woman lying next to him. Another man's wife, but one he felt connected to. It wasn't something that made sense, and if he tried to explain it to Julie Ciskowski, she'd tell him he was a fool and she'd probably be right to do so. Still, there were worse things to make a fool of yourself for.

"You're a beautiful woman," Maitland said, thinking on his feet. "But I've got enough enemies right now. I don't need to worry about your husband too. Besides . . ."

"Besides what?"

"Nothing."

"No, go ahead."

"Well, part of me wonders if you'd be doing it to get back at Cason and Specht." Maitland said, "I'm sorry, but it has occurred to me."

After a moment, Julie said, "Well, you might be onto something there. Would it make a difference to you?"

"Yeah, I'm afraid it would."

"How come?"

"Well . . . I don't know. It would be awkward and . . . there has to be some discourse."

"Isn't talking about it awkward?"

"No," Maitland said. "Not so much."

"Well," Julie said, "it's a start."

She stood up.

She said, "What do you want me to do? I mean, what do you want from the department?"

"I need Jukie Blake's address."

"What are you going to do? Never mind, don't tell me."

"Will you get it for me?"

"Yeah." She walked to the door. "I'll call you in the morning." She stood at the door a moment before she walked out. "Discourse," she said, shaking her head.

THIRTY-SEVEN

She called him early, about seven-thirty, waking him up.

"Evan?"

"Yeah."

"You got a pen?"

"Just a minute . . . okay."

She gave him an address and he wrote it down.

"Okay," he said.

"Evan," she said, "be careful now. Those guys like to torture and kill."

"I'll remember that."

He placed his next call. Charlie answered on the third ring.

"Mead."

"Charlie, it's Evan. Listen, I need a car. Just for a couple of days. Your brother still own the used car lot?"

"Yeah. You need it today?"

"Yeah. Soon as possible."

"Okay. The lot's on Diversey and Eighth, remember?"

"I remember. Can you meet me there in an hour?"

"Sure. Anything in particular?"

"No, nothing special. Just a car. I'll see you in an hour."

Thirty minutes later an MTA bus stopped on Diversey and Maitland stepped off of it. He walked without his cane the block and a half to Max's Quality Cars. In his right hand he held a blue gym bag.

Charlie Mead was on the lot, standing by a maroon '96 Monte Carlo.

"Morning, Charlie."

"Morning, Evan."

Charlie Mead gestured to the car. He was uncomfortable and self-conscious, a self-made man acting like a valet. Maitland knew that Charlie felt guilty about Maitland getting shot and not getting paid. Charlie had not offered to pay Maitland's fee regardless of his failure to bring McDermott back because of the injury. Maitland had not asked him to pay and he never would. Charlie retained him for a job, but Charlie could not have known how dangerous the job could be. It wasn't Charlie's fault, but Charlie was a human being and he felt bad about how things had turned out.

Charlie said, "It's got Maryland tags. They're bogus and they can't be traced back to anyone."

Maitland said, "Good. I should have it back tomorrow."

"No hurry, man."

Maitland got in the Monte Carlo, started it and pulled off the lot. Charlie Mead watched as the car merged into the morning traffic and faded out of sight.

THIRTY-EIGHT

Jukie lived in an upscale high-rise apartment building near the North Shore. It was called the Liberty Towers and it was down the street from the building Ann Landers used to live in. The Liberty Towers had been designed by Frank Lloyd Wright and it was tall and glassy and glacial. There was parking underneath and the tenants drove out from the structure through a faded yellow automatic door. There were two sets of doors — one for egress and another for ingress.

Maitland sat in the Monte Carlo across the street from the doors until he saw a silver 1987 Jaguar XJ6 come out.

The Jag stopped at the end of the drive, paused, then turned left into traffic and moved off. Jukie Blake was driving it.

He's got taste in cars, Maitland thought. Eighty-seven was the last year of the XJ6's Pininfarina design. They may have made them more reliable after that, but they never made them as pretty.

Maitland drove the Monte Carlo ten blocks away and parked it. He walked back to the Liberty Towers carrying the gym bag.

He took his time, waiting for the right moment, then maneuvered himself behind the trash Dumpsters near the exit garage. After a few minutes, the door opened and a Cadillac SUV came out. Maitland went into the garage before the door came back down.

Trevor Jim reached Jukie at their Gold Street club, one of their business fronts. The Raetown posse funneled some of the profits from their crackhouses and gun sales into the place. As clubs went, it was fairly low key, opting to retain the flavor of the island. On Saturdays they played Bob Marley, the Platters, the O-Jays singing "Love Train."

Trevor Jim said, "We on our way back. We didn't find the woman. We don't find nothing."

Jukie said, "Hmmm."

Trevor Jim said, "The woman's husband says she left him, went back to Chicago."

"Anything else?"

"No. That's all he know."

Jukie said, "Chicago's a big city."

"We'll find her," Trevor Jim said.

They finished their conversation, both men feeling uneasy but not wanting to give voice to their separate anxieties. For his part, Jukie felt things were getting complicated. He knew that loyalty was a scarce commodity in posses. What's more, he knew that Trevor knew he knew. The police lean on a soldier of the posse — perhaps arrest him for low-level dealing — and generally he'll flip on the leader. If Mr. Maitland fingered Jukie to the police and they came after him, Jukie wasn't quite sure what he would do. He could take it like a man, stand up and see if they could make a case stick against him.

Or, he could turn himself in and flip on Trevor and Maurice. Maybe draw a five-year sentence. Do it right, and maybe Trevor wouldn't get the chance to kill him. See if the feds would relocate him to California or some other place warmer than this cold, raggedy motherfucker.

Or, he could bond out and skip to Florida then catch a plane or a boat for home. Or, maybe England. He had a brother in England. Jeffrey, nine years older than him. He remembered watching Jeffrey getting on a ship bound for England. He hadn't seen him since. Jukie had been eleven years old at the time. And watching the ship sail out of Kingston had been another painful episode in his painful youth.

Jukie grew up near a small town called

Cave Valley. He had a brother and a sister. His father was a farmer that, like many at the time, had resorted to growing ganja to survive. It kept the family fed and the profits went to the city dealers. And then the Americans decided to declare war on drugs and make the farmers suffer most of all. Jukie remembered the helicopters landing in their fields, a soldier pointing an M-16 at his father and mother as they set fire to the crop. His little sister crying as the family's livelihood went up in smoke.

The politicians came to the communities later, promising to make everything better. The JLP candidates saying things were going to change. The Jamaican Labor Party, though the candidates liked to tell the farmers the acronym meant Jesus Loving People. But nothing changed and Jukie drifted to Kingston and joined the Raetown Posse. He spent his early teens in filthy neighborhood tenements, people pissing on the ground and shitting in a bucket . . . the Kingston ghetto where running water is for the rich. He lost his virginity to a prostitute in the Seaview Club. At one of the weekly street draws in Raetown, Jukie got in an argument with another fellah over a girl and Jukie shot him. Fortunately, the fellah turned out to be a nobody that didn't belong to any gang worth noting. Jukie's coldbloodedness gained the respect of Trevor Jim Collins. Trevor Jim moved him up to a higher rank within the posse and then eventually took him to Chicago.

It was silly to think of it now. You could say it was, what, *simpler* then. Back then, they were so young and nobody ever gave serious thought to dying. That they would one day live in high-dollar condominiums in America and drive expensive automobiles was inconceivable. The focus back then had been short-term. Like most men of poverty and degradation and internal war, Jukie had thought of the future only in terms of days. He had not been prepared to think long-term. He used the posse to escape the war-like conditions of his own country. But then they moved to another country and just continued the war there. Killing members of rival posses in a North American city, raiding the crackhouses of rival dealers. Violence begetting more violence. Things hadn't really changed. They had only gotten money.

He thought, now where do you go? You can kill Maitland. But he was proving himself not so easy to kill. Three men dead now. A white man who didn't look like much when you first saw him. Not like

Schwarzenegger or Stallone or Eastwood or any of those other white supermen he had grown up watching on the screen. But three men were dead and he was alive. Trevor wanted the fellah dead, but he wasn't giving any suggestions on how to do it. Not lately, anyway.

Jukie was not educated, but he was smart. Yet for all his intelligence, it disconcerted him that a fellah he had put a bullet in was still alive. He wasn't quite ready to believe that the fellah was some sort of ghost, a spirit rather than a man. But he couldn't quite dismiss the possibility either. When he thought of it that way, he was embarrassed and slightly ashamed. Thoughts like that kept the black man beneath the white man, he thought. He could not admit such an insecurity to Trevor or Maurice because they would accuse him of being a fool, a self-hating nigger who deep down believed the white man was superior. Jesus, they would probably kill him in disgust. It would do no good to explain that what he felt was not a racial inferiority complex, but a suspicion. Bad karma, nothing more. A fellah gets shot in the chest and lives, maybe it's best to leave him alone. Live and let live.

But how do you explain it to Trevor? How do you explain that and live?

★ ★ ★

Maitland hid in the parking garage behind the vending machines around the corner from the elevator. In his hand he held a riot baton he had taken out of his gym bag.

Law enforcement instructors teach that head blows with the riot baton are at the far end of the "use-of-force continuum." A well-placed strike can split a man's head like a cantaloupe, they say. And even Chicago police officers are only to use it in times of extreme emergency. You need to kill someone, you draw your sidearm. Don't use the riot baton.

Standing behind a coke machine with the intent to ambush a citizen, it struck Maitland as ironic that he would remember his police training. Still, he needed to focus on something, keep his thoughts going to stave off the boredom. He told himself that he did not want to kill Jukie Blake. He did not know with absolute certainty that Jukie had sent the Italians after him. He had nothing solid. No tape of a conversation between Blake and the men in the mattress shop. He had no direct evidence. But the indirect evidence was substantial. Charles Manson had been convicted on less. Though he lacked absolute certainty, he knew that the Jamaicans had sent the Italians.

Jesus, he thought. Jamaicans. Italians. Like he was getting caught up in some sort of colonial war. What next, the Greeks? Okay, it was silly to think of it along those lines. They hadn't come after him because he was of Germanic stock or acting on behalf of the Crown. So he wasn't going after them because they were black or Mediterranean. He remembered an old cop once telling him that the District Attorney's office used to have an internal *written directive* instructing the prosecutors to pull blacks and Jews off the juries. Times had changed. Maybe.

Standing alone in the dark and shadows, thinking because there was nothing else to do. Think and wait. He could try to control the thinking and stay cool. But we can't not think of a blue polar bear when someone tells us not to.

Four men, he thought. Four men he had killed now. And he was worried about it. He was worried about himself. Maitland was not especially religious. If there was a hell, he figured he was going there for any number of reasons. He believed that a man was what he did, not what he said he was or thought he was. A murderer could be a good

253

husband and father, but he would still be a murderer. He knew he was a killer because he had killed. He did not want to think he was a murderer. The soldier who killed in war, did he think he was a murderer? If he fired his rifle or dropped the bomb without hatred for the Jap or the Kraut or the Arab did it make any difference? And if he did feel hatred in his heart, was it fair for the civilian to judge him for feeling it? Was it easier for the soldier to feel hatred, to envision the enemy as something less than human? Did he even have the time to make such considerations?

The reality was, he was alive and four men were dead. They needed to die in order for him to live. It had been necessary. Because it had been necessary, he did not feel shame over it. But he did feel regret. Perhaps it would be different had he killed them in war, but he hadn't. He had killed them on highways and in homes. On American soil. They had not been terrorists seeking to destroy the nation, just losers, small-time criminals that had tried to kill him. He regretted that the path of his life had led to killing. He regretted that he was not one of those men he had seen in Lincoln Park watching their children playing soccer on Saturdays. A life without blood or ugliness or violence. A life without the fear that some gross, dark part of you might take satisfaction in putting an end to a man's life.

It was when he thought of the men in the Lexus that he became frightened. There had been a moment when he had a hunch that the men in the Lexus would throw in the towel and leave him alone. It was after he had battered them a few times. Conceivably, they might have been willing to peel off the interstate at the next exit ramp and call it a day. He would never really know. Because he hadn't let them go. He had given them that final push off the road. Then they had died. So, was it self-defense or was it vengeance? Was it to punish them for having the audacity to try to kill him? He liked to think it was self-defense, but he couldn't really be sure. It had all happened so fast. And self-defense was a difficult concept to define. The woman kills her abusive husband while he's asleep in his bed. Her defense is that he was going to kill her sooner or later and you cops won't take an interest until I'm dead. And she's probably right. But to kill a man while he's asleep? Do you file charges on her or let her go? Should she be so morally opposed to killing that she has to sacrifice her own life?

He remembered waxing this sort of philosophy when he had killed Ronnie Ellis. But it was different with Ronnie. He knew Ronnie. He liked him, in fact. Ronnie was a high-level crank dealer. Selling death and destruction, but he was a charmer and he could make you laugh. Maitland went undercover and got close to him. But to get the man's trust you have to befriend him. They didn't train you for that. They didn't prepare you for growing to like someone like Ronnie Ellis. He remembered Ronnie greeting one of his lackeys, saying, "There's Fred Sanford," then with great timing, pointing to another, saying, "and there's Grady." The resemblance actually had been pretty much there too. It was hard not to like Ronnie.

But somehow Ronnie got on to Maitland. Maitland never did find out how, but one night Ronnie confronted him by sticking a gun in his face, asking him if he was a narc. Maitland answered with his narc lies and for a while he thought he was going to convince Ronnie he was mistaken, but then saw that it wasn't working and he was going to die. Ronnie was cranked at the time and was not concentrating as well as he could be. If he had been, he would have probably lived. As it was, Maitland made a grab for Ronnie's gun. They grappled for a few moments and

Ronnie knocked him against a wall. Then Ronnie squeezed off a shot but it hit the wall inches from Maitland's face. Maitland drew and shot Ronnie twice in the chest.

Ronnie fell to the ground. Maitland took Ronnie's gun and threw it across the room, but held Ronnie's hand as the life bled out of him. Ronnie said, "Man, you shot me," more disappointed than angry. He died minutes later.

When he thought about Ronnie, Maitland remembered the time Ronnie had been on the phone, concerned about something. Ronnie had said, "I love you, mama." After he hung up, Maitland had asked him how his mother was. She wasn't good, he'd said. Her second kidney surgery and it looked real bad. Maitland had said, "I'm sorry, Ronnie." He'd meant it too. A month after that conversation, he took the woman's son's life. He told Ronnie he was sorry then, too.

Christ. Undercover work was not for the faint of heart. It was better left to the modern day Inspector Javerts that believe clear-cut violations of law remove any trace of humanity from the lawbreaker. It had been hard then. But it was getting easier now. It was the getting easier part that worried Maitland.

The garage door opened.

Maitland peered out from between the vending machines to see the grill of the XJ6 come into view. It was Jukie. The tires squealed in the dark as the Jag found its place.

Maitland heard the engine cut and the door slam. He retreated further into the shadows.

Footsteps on concrete. Coming closer, then closer. He could hear the man's breathing.

And then Jukie walked past the space between the vending machines and the elevator. Maitland saw him but he did not see Maitland.

Jukie pressed the up button. Soon the elevator dinged its arrival.

Maitland stepped out, the baton in one hand, the gym bag in the other. He dropped the gym bag on the ground as Jukie focused his surprised look on him. Maitland drove the end of the baton into Jukie's solar plexus. Jukie doubled over, gasping, and Maitland grabbed the back of his jacket and drove him into the elevator, half running, getting the momentum up as they moved inside and Maitland slammed Jukie's head into the mirrored wall of the elevator box. The glass shattered and Jukie slumped to the ground. Maitland bent over Jukie, found a gun in his jacket pocket and took it from him.

Maitland saw the gym bag outside the elevator. It had the duct tape inside which he had planned to use to bind Jukie's arms and legs. But if he stepped out the elevator doors might shut and he'd lose Jukie. So he pressed the button that closed the doors and hit the elevator switch to floor five, all the while holding Jukie's gun on Jukie. He pressed the red stop button between the third and fourth floor.

Maitland said, "Sit up."

Jukie sat up, staring at him, putting him in context as best he could. There was a gash in his forehead, blood streaking down the side of his face.

Maitland backed to the opposite side of the elevator.

He said, "Keep your back against the wall. Stay on the floor."

Maitland took a handkerchief from his pocket and tossed it to the man on the floor. Jukie picked it up, put it to the gash in his head. He smiled.

"What are you waiting for?" Jukie said.

Maitland said, "I didn't come here to kill you."

"I see," Jukie said. He gestured with the

handkerchief. "We de savages, you de civilized white man, uh?"

"I'm the same color as those muckers you sent to kill me, b'woy."

Jukie laughed. A legitimate laugh, not an attempt to psych him. "Man," Jukie said, "you a pretty cool cat. Like, ah, Lee Marvin. Huh?"

"Lee Marvin? Was he on the 'Mod Squad'?"

"No, mon. He not on the 'Mod Squad.' The white fellah on that show, you never see him noplace else. You like the girl on the show?"

"Peggy Lipton. Yeah, I liked her. She's still good-looking."

"She married to a bredda, you know that?

"No shit. Who's that?"

"Quincy Jones. He a musician."

"Yeah?"

"Yeah. He wrote the theme to 'Sanford and Son.' Whuh-whuh-whuh-wah-wah, wah-wah." Jukie said, "Does that bother you, good-looking white woman married to a black fellah?"

"Oh, yeah. Keeps me awake at night," Maitland said. "Right now, I got bigger problems. I got a Jamaican posse making a fucking mess of my life. I was wondering if you could tell me why?"

"Who say we trying to kill you?"

Maitland frowned. "Hey, I thought we were friends. You gonna lie to me?"

"What proof you have?"

"I got a lung missing. You shot it out. I got a couple of Italians I know you do business with trying to kill me. That's all the proof I need."

"Yeah? What do the police say?"

"I'm not sure actually. I'm here on my behalf, not theirs."

Jukie seemed to study him for a moment. He said, "You come here to make peace?"

"Sort of," Maitland said. "I've got a settlement offer."

"Settle what?"

"This dispute between me and you. Me and your people."

"What can you offer us?"

"An end to this."

Jukie pondered it, realized the man was serious. He said, "What if we say, it ends the way we want it to end."

Maitland gestured with the gun. He said, "It hasn't yet, has it?"

Jukie said, "What do you want?"

"You cost me a thirty-thousand-dollar fee when you took Barry away from me. I've lost a car and a lung. If I were to sue someone in court for that, I'd get a half million easy. I'll settle for two hundred thousand."

Jukie looked at him in disbelief. "You are crazy. Do you think Trevor Jim will actually give you that kind of money?"

"It's not a gift. It's payment of a debt."

"You killed one of his men. He could just as easily ask you for money."

"That was in self-defense. You know that. You were there. Besides, my hands were clean. I was there to bring a man back pursuant to the law. You were there to kill him."

"Not just."

Maitland thought back to the little pillbox house in Oklahoma. He said, "You said Barry stole money from you. How much did he take?"

"A lot."

"Enough for you to chase him. Was he laundering money for you guys?"

"Barry got cheeky. He forgot who his friends were."

"I'll ask you again: how much did he take?"

"He took about eight hundred thousand."

"Wow. That's a lot of money. Did you ever get it back?"

"No."

Maitland thought for a moment. Then he asked what happened to Barry McDermott.

"You know," Jukie said, "he got away. We didn't have a very good day then."

"To where, the front door?"

"I don't know nothing about that."

Jukie looked at Maitland for a long time then. And then Jukie smiled. It was a smile of satisfaction and it was unnerving.

"Mr. Maitland, I know something about human beings. And right now I think you a lot of bullshit. I don't think you want money from us at all. You are an ex-policeman, but a policeman all the same. A law-abiding citizen. You don't take money from me before, but now you offer to . . . ? No. No, it will not work. I not going to give you nothing."

"You sure about that?" Maitland said, but it was slipping from him.

Jukie said, "Let me ask you something: you been shot and yet the police don't come looking for me. Why is that?"

"Just a matter of time."

"Really? Where are they? I don't see them. Where are you hiding them?" He was smiling wide now. "I think you all alone. I tell you, I would not want to be in your shoes right now."

"Why is that?"

"Oh, stop with the nonsense. Mr.

Maitland, you not ready for this side of the world. Over here, we don't knock fellahs over the head and ask for money. We just kill them and take what we want. Sometimes we torture them. That sort of thing, it's not in you. I know."

"Don't be too sure of yourself," Maitland said. He regretted saying it so quickly, protesting too much.

"Then shoot me," Jukie said. "Do it now. Send a message to my people: Don't fuck wit' Mr. Maitland." Jukie smiled again. "Come on. Kill an unarmed man and let them know what a coldhearted fellah they are dealing with."

A few long seconds passed. The two men stared at each other and the only sound was the buzz of the electricity keeping the lights in the elevator on. Maitland didn't move.

"All right," Maitland said. "You got me. I don't want your money. It's brought you nothing but bloodshed."

"Mr. Maitland, our whole life is bloodshed. With or without money."

"You ask for my pity now?"

"Never would I seek pity. Least of all from you."

It was not something that Maitland could understand. He was the one who'd been shot, after all. Maitland said, "Then walk away. All of you, just walk away and leave me alone."

"If it were up to me, that's what we would do. But it's not up to me."

"Can you persuade Collins to back off?" He hated having to ask that question because it might make him look weak and desperate. He certainly felt that way.

Jukie shook his head. It occurred to Maitland that he might be an honest man, in his way. "I don't think so," Jukie said. "He a very black and white sort of fellah. You a witness and you killed one of his men. If you were a cop, it would be different. But you not anymore. You just a man."

Maitland released the stop button and opened the elevator doors at the next floor. Before he got off, Jukie spoke to him.

"What do you want me tell Trevor?"

"Tell him whatever you like," Maitland said.

THIRTY-NINE

Trevor Jim was fucking with him, acting like he didn't understand certain parts of what he was saying but really making him repeat things for the purpose of making him feel like an hysterical old woman. It was winding Jukie up and he had to be patient and cool so he wouldn't slam Trevor Jim's head into the coffee table.

They were in the living room of Jukie's apartment. Jukie lay on the couch, holding an ice pack to his head as Trevor Jim sat in the dark leather chair Jukie used for watching DVDs. Maurice remained standing, giving Jukie the eye here and there for lying on the couch and not showing the proper respect.

Trevor Jim said, "Go back to the part before you got on the elevator. You say he was waiting in there for you?"

"No, mon. That's not what I said. I said he hit me before we got on the elevator."

"Why did you let him hit you?"

"I didn't let him, Trevor. He just came out from the corner and did it."

"I see."

There was a patronizing tone there. Had

266

another man spoken to him like that, Jukie would have killed him. Jukie was getting sick of it, sick of responding to the man's stupid questions and smart bwoy comments, so he decided to go on the offensive himself. He said, "Well?"

Trevor Jim looked surprised. "Well what?" he said.

Jukie said, "What are you going to do?"

"What do you mean?"

"You going to pay him the two hundred thousand?"

Jukie knew the answer already. He knew that Trevor Jim would never give the bounty hunter two hundred thousand. He also knew that Maitland didn't even really want it. He just wanted enough information to get them all indicted. Trying to play head games with old Jukie, the fool. But Jukie was pissed off at Trevor now and he wanted him to believe that Jukie thought he might be woman enough to contemplate paying the money.

It was intended to insult Trevor, and it did. But Trevor Jim kept his cool. He eyed Jukie, seeking an overt sign of insolence. But Jukie maintained his schoolboy expression. And then Trevor Jim threw it back at him, saying, "What do you think I should do?"

Jukie made a gesture. "It's your money," he said. "Do with it what you like."

"I have not met the fellah. You tell me what you think of him."

Jukie shrugged. "He might be crazy. Or stupid. Or he may mean what he say."

"He can mean what he say *and* be crazy and stupid."

"He's killed three men already."

"So what is that to us?"

"Well, it can be bad for us. He used to be a policeman, but he not a policeman anymore. So he knows what to do, how to shoot a man and keep going. But he's not held in by the American policeman rules. He is unrestrained. In a way, it is like back home."

"You think he would do that?"

"Yes."

"Then we have to find him first, torture him and then kill him."

FORTY

Well, Maitland thought, that was a fucking debacle.

Sitting in his apartment thinking about it, he tried to see if something good had come of it, tried to see if he was better off having whaled on Jukie than if he had left him alone. The more he thought about it, the more he had to conclude that he had fucked up. The running into the posse in Oklahoma City, that had just been bad luck. He could not have known what sort of bad, dangerous characters Barry McDermott would attract. But this afternoon — going down to Jukie's apartment and waiting for him — well, that had been Maitland's idea alone. That was something he had chosen.

Maitland took it and played it back, like a Monday morning coach, and picked out his mistakes.

Mistake number 1: He had overplayed his hand. He had started out talking about money and at first Jukie had believed he was serious. But then he had started asking cop questions. Too many, too obvious. And he blew it. Blew his own goddam cover like a

269

pimple-faced rookie. He never would have made such a mistake back in the day. How had he let that happen? How did he let that lowlife smoke him out?

Perhaps it was because it had been too long since he had done undercover work, too long since he had been a cop. Go out into the civilian world and sell furniture, you may make some money but you'll lose your seedy edge. Like an actor who had played himself on a long-running television sitcom and forgot how to act on stage. *I think you a lot of bullshit.*

Which led to mistake number 2: Underestimating Jukie Blake. Thinking about it now, Maitland almost admired the fuckhead. Not many men can call bullshit on a guy holding a gun on them. But Jukie had. And now things were worse than before. Now Jukie knew the cops had left Maitland out to dry. He didn't know why, but he knew all the same. And now Maitland's life was on the order of a penny stock.

What do I do now? he thought. What now?

He could drive down to Trevor Jim's batcave on a day of business, go in the front door with his .38 and his .45 and start blasting until they were all dead. Maybe

270

he'd even be able to pull it off. But then he'd be indicted for murder. Terry Specht would testify that Maitland had acted in character, wanting to eliminate all his co-conspirators.

But it was no use anyway. Even if the District Attorney's office gave him the sort of pre-approved dispensation Janet Reno seemed to give the ATF before they massacred the Branch Davidians at Waco, he doubted he would have the stomach to carry out such raw butchery. Jukie had figured that out. It was one thing to kill a man who's blazing away at you with a shotgun, quite another to carry out a premeditated act of murder. Or murders.

It was all so upside down. Terry Specht. Terry fucking Specht had put him here. He had used his influence and guile to shut down any prosecution of these guys. Specht had made Maitland a suspect. And now the real menaces to society were going to kill him.

Maitland had the cynical view of human nature that is inherent in all former police officers. But even he had trouble believing that Terry would intentionally do this to him. Was it because Terry was pissed off about what had happened years ago? Would he hold a grudge that long? Or, did Terry honestly believe that Maitland was dirty, was corrupt, was a killer? Was Terry honestly mistaken?

Oh, the hell with it. In the end, what difference does it make? Good faith or bad, Terry's fucked me.

He thought back to when he first met Terry Specht. It was at his internal affairs administrative interview. It took place the day after Maitland had killed Ronnie Ellis. Maitland thought it was just a routine procedure. But then Terry started asking questions without first reading the *Garrity* warning and Maitland stopped him.

The transcript of the taped interview was later provided to the arbitrator.

Maitland: Wait a minute, we need to get *Garrity* on the record.
Specht: Why?
Maitland: Uh, so I don't waive my Fifth Amendment rights.
Specht: You got nothing to hide, do you?
Maitland: No. But proper procedure is that the *Garrity* warning is given.
Specht: Why don't you just tell me what happened? That's an order.
Maitland: It's an unlawful order, sir. You do not have the authority to order me to waive my Fifth Amendment

rights. Respectfully, I request that it be read into the record and I'll answer whatever questions you have.

Realizing he had no choice but to comply with the law, Terry eventually gave the warning on the record and began his interrogation. But the arbitrator would later ask Lieutenant Specht why he tried to force Maitland to waive his Fifth Amendment rights. The *Garrity* warning specifically allowed the lieutenant to ask all the questions he liked so long as he assured the subject of the investigation that his Fifth Amendment right not to incriminate himself would be guarded and that nothing he said would be used for the purpose of filing criminal charges. Was there some reason he had for trying to force the officer to waive it? Terry, sitting in the witness chair, said he just didn't think it was important. The arbitrator looked at him with something like wonder.

Maitland figured the truthful answer to that question was that Terry simply wanted to force him to resign. That is, get enough information out of him and then threaten to have him criminally prosecuted unless he resigned. As nasty internal police tactics went, it was not an unusual ploy. The problem was, Terry lacked the imagination to attempt it with any subtlety.

Maitland won that battle. The arbitrator ordered him reinstated with all back pay and benefits. But the department won in the end by making his return so unwelcome he eventually *did* resign. And now Terry Specht was paying him back in spades. Maybe if he had said something to Terry afterwards. Sought him out after the arbitration and said something like, "Hey, no hard feelings. I know you were just doing your job." But he hadn't. And, truth be told, if his closest, most trusted friend at the time had even suggested he do such a thing Maitland would have told him to fuck off. He felt then that Terry had done something despicable, destructive and cowardly in trying to ruin him and under no circumstances would he try to repair any rift with the man.

He still felt that way now. But he wondered if it was worth smiling at Terry after the thing was finished. It was the same tone, the same attitude he had displayed when he had told the yokel cops in Oklahoma City, "It was just that easy." It was the very spice of life to twist people like that, but, shit on a stick, you paid for it in the end.

Well, what was done was done. He didn't have the means to go back and fix any of it now. An apology now to Terry Specht would only engender contempt. And the withdrawal of his "demand" to the posse would have pretty much the same effect. Jukie would either report what Maitland had done to Trevor or not. If he were lucky, Trevor would shrug it off. Odds of that outcome were unlikely. Maitland had worked in undercover enough to learn that Jamaican posses took vengeance and respect even more seriously than their American gangster counterparts. And by demanding money, he had shown disrespect.

Which he had intended. But he had hoped to get some decent information in exchange for it. With luck, enough information to take back to Julie Ciskowski and get her to persuade people that didn't have their head up their ass to go after these guys. But it had gone nowhere. And now he was in more danger. Over what? Some jerk-off that couldn't keep his hands off the young stuff. A thief, stealing money from some very dangerous men, bringing those same dangerous men and Terry Specht into his previously peaceful life.

The money, money. . . .

They never got the money.

They never got the money that Barry stole from them.

Hmmm. Jukie had said that much.

Where was the money?

Jukie said Barry had taken about $800,000. Where was it? Barry took $800,000 and went down to Oklahoma. The breddas caught up with him and killed him but they never found the money.

Where was it?

His car?

No. They would have looked there.

His house?

No. They would have looked there too. They went to his house and killed the girl. Cinnamon Barefoot. A stripper and girlfriend, dead before she reached thirty.

Linda O'Connell?

No. He wouldn't have left it with her. Nothing pointed that way.

When Barry ran, he took the money with him. The money went down to Oklahoma.

It didn't come back. Not with the posse anyway.

"Kittycat," Maitland said.

FORTY-ONE

Jeff Johnson didn't mind wearing the uniform driving back and forth to the base. He was fighting in a popular war and people gave him respect. Old men nodded at him at the grocery stores. Fat ladies thanked him for what he was doing and told him it was good to have him home. They'd ask him if his tour was done and he'd say, "No, ma'am. I'm shipping out next week." He wished a good-looking babe would say things like that to him, then patriotically offer herself for the night. But it hadn't happened. Ungrateful bitches.

At bars, young men would come up and ask what it was like, being out there in the desert shooting at people. Jeff would say he couldn't really describe it to someone who hadn't been there. He wouldn't tell them that he hadn't actually been doing the fighting. He felt no shame in not running to the front. Only the young ones wanted to be in the shit. Or the crazy ones. At twenty-nine, Jeff was older than most of the soldiers who had crossed the borders into Iraq and Afghanistan. The soldier would understand that. But the civilians wouldn't understand shit. They'd seen movies with forty-five-year-old Tom Hanks playing the captain leading men into northern France. Yeah, the heads exploding like watermelons with M-80's stuffed inside, that was real enough. But the average infantry officer was twenty-four. The military liked them young. Not just because they were faster and stronger. But because they were young too. Young enough not to question duty, honor and country. Young enough not to understand that life is for the living.

Jeff had not called the police since being terrorized by the Jamaicans. He didn't know what they were after specifically. And some part of him hoped they'd catch up with that cunt wife of his and give her what she had coming to her. He tried to convince himself that was the only reason. But he was scared too. Scared of what they might do to him. They were criminals. Hardcore mother-fuckers who'd cut him up like salad and not blink an eye while doing it. Plus, if he called the police they'd end up giving the hard-on. *What was your wife involved in? Why did she leave you? How is it you're associated with these black drug dealers?* The brass didn't like their noncoms getting in domestic troubles. Jeff thought that after he got back from his next tour, maybe he'd drive up to Chicago with a couple of trigger-happy jarheads and find those niggers himself. Fill their black asses with M-16 rounds. Yeah, that'd be nice. That would be the way to handle it. Hell. He might even do it.

On his way back from Tinker, he bought a twelve-pack of Bud at the grocery store. Then swung by the Taco Bell to pick up a couple of macho-meat burritos. He drove home and opened the first can, used another to wash down the grub. He drank a couple more while he watched television. It was a movie that he had come in the middle of, something with Sandra Bullock chasing serial killers. It didn't make too much sense and after about twenty minutes he gave up on it and switched to CNN to watch some blonde girl defend Joseph McCarthy. It threw him for a loop; he thought at first she might have been one of those skanky bitches from "Friends," being humorous.

The telephone rang.

Jeff let it ring a couple more times before picking it up.

"Yeah."

"Hello. Who is this?"

Jeff said, "Who is this?"

"Evan Maitland. I'm a bail enforcement agent from Chicago."

Jeff's heart quickened as the black guys with knives came into his head. This had to have something to do with it.

Jeff said, "What do you want?"

"I need to speak to Diane."

"She's not here."

"Are you her husband?"

"No."

Maitland paused. "Who are you then?"

"Sergeant Jeff Johnson. USAF. Who the fuck are you?"

"I already told you," Maitland said. "Listen, this is a law enforcement matter. I need to speak to her."

"Well, like I said, she's not here."

"Do you know where she is?"

"She went back to Chicago."

"She did?" Maitland said, "When?"

"I don't know. A couple of weeks ago."

"Do you know where to reach her?"

"She didn't leave a forwarding address. Maybe I'll get divorce papers in the mail. Then I'll know." Jeff Johnson said, "Why don't you call me back then."

Maitland figured the guy was drunk and he could probably get away with blurring the distinction between private citizen and federal agent.

"Hey, asshole," Maitland said, "don't get smart with me. Obstructing a police investigation is a crime."

There was a pause and Maitland waited for the guy to take it. Or hang up the phone.

Maitland said, his tone hard, "You still there?"

"Yes, sir."

"Okay, then. Now where is she?"

"Really, sir. I don't know. If I did, I would tell you."

"How do you know she's in Chicago?"

"She told me that much. Anyway, where else would she go?"

"All right. I'm going to give you my cell number. You hear from her, you call me immediately. You understand?"

"Yes, sir." Jeff hesitated for a moment. "Sir?"

"Yeah?"

"Are you going to find those guys?"

In his home, Maitland leaned forward in his chair.

"What guys?" he said.

"Those black guys."

Maitland said, "Who are you talking about?"

"You know, those Island ni— Black guys. Talk like they're from Jamaica."

"Jesus Christ. Did you see them?"

"Yes."

"When?"

"A couple of days ago."

"What did they want?"

"They were looking for money."

Maitland said, "Jeff, did you call the police?"

"Uh . . ."

"You've got to call the police. You hear me? Call them ASAP. You don't report it, I will."

"All right, I will."

"Do it soon, Jeff."

"Hey," Jeff said. "I thought you were the police?"

Maitland said, "Chicago."

FORTY-TWO

Jay Jackson's voice boomed over the telephone.

"Evan Maitland," he said. "I heard about you."

"Yeah?" Maitland said. "What did you hear?"

"I heard you were dead."

"No."

"Actually, I heard you got shot. In Oklahoma City?"

"That's right. Thanks for the flowers."

"Hey, anything for my friends."

He hadn't sent flowers or even called and Maitland knew it. Maitland would have felt embarrassed if he had. They did not have that sort of friendship. Maitland said, "I need a favor."

"Ask me anything."

"I need you to arrest some people."

"I can't help you."

"You haven't even heard what I got to say."

"All right," Jay said. "Tell me who you want arrested. Then I'll say no."

"Raetown Posse. Heard of them?"

283

"Oh, yeah. Mean boys. Smart too."

"They're the ones that shot me."

"Yeah? Wasn't that in Oklahoma City?"

"Yeah."

"That's their jurisdiction then."

"We're all back in Chicago now. Besides," Evan said. "They killed a woman here. Her name was Cinnamon Barefoot. A Chicago detective named Julie Ciskowski was handling it, but she was pulled off the case."

"Why?"

"It's a long story. But you can subpoena her files."

"Yeah . . . sounds like I'd be stepping on some toes, though. You got evidence of trafficking?"

Maitland sighed. He liked Jay Jackson. Even if he didn't, if he misled or deceived him, he'd never be able to ask for his help again.

"No," Maitland said. "Not directly anyway. Barry McDermott — the skipper — it looks like he stole money from the posse and ran down to Oklahoma City. They caught up with him and no one's seen him since. They crossed state lines to do it." Maitland said, "That gives the FBI jurisdiction."

"Yeah," Jay said. "But you know how

284

they are. Like to get all their ducks in a row before they start shooting. You throwing all this at me now for the first time."

"What if the money was found?"

"What if it was? Unless it's got a brick of coke in the bag, my dick ain't gonna get hard."

Maitland thought for a moment. "What if the money had McDermott's prints on it? Even just some of it."

"What if it did?"

"We could tie it back to the posse. It'd be something."

"Yeah," Jay said. "But they got to claim it. They can look at it, say they never seen it before."

"Can you do anything?"

"Well . . . let me chuck it around here for a while. I'll see what I can do."

Maitland kept his irritation to himself. Fucking feds. Unless one of their own got killed, they seemed to have trouble taking an interest in murder. They wanted drug buys and sells. Product. Or serial killers, traveling across state lines and chopping people into little pieces. The posse was capable of that sort of brutality as well as any monster who started out watching porn flicks in his basement. But for them brutality was mostly a means to an end. Too

285

workmanlike to interest the psych majors at Behavioral Science.

Still, it wasn't Jay's fault. He was only following company policy. Plus, though he wouldn't say it out loud, Maitland knew that Jay would have trouble convincing the brass to act on the word of a disgraced ex-cop. If they called Julie and only Julie, he might be okay. If they called Terry Specht, he'd get shit.

"Okay," Maitland said. "Say, can you get an address for me?"

"Who?"

"Her name is Diane Johnson. Or Diane Creasey. I think she just moved back to Chicago. Her e-mail address is DKittyKat at aol.com."

"Okay."

"ASAP?"

"Yeah. I'll call you."

"Thanks, man."

Maitland hung up the phone.

It was almost five o'clock. Shadows lengthened into his apartment windows. It was quiet inside — his radio and television turned off and the city giving its background. He had that vaguely guilty feeling of being home too early. He had called Bianca this morning and told her he would not be in until after lunch. He hadn't called her after that. Almost five o'clock and he would not be going in today. He wished it was not so late. Were it earlier he would drive down to the store. Not because he wanted to work but because it might make him feel less frightened. Activity might take his mind off death threats and gangsters.

But it was no good. A retreat into the store would probably bring little comfort. Making believe it was three weeks earlier when it wasn't. Three weeks earlier and he was alive and bored and restless and people weren't trying to kill him. Now he had excitement to spare and it sucked. And he had placed Bianca in danger. The thought that she could have been walking out of the antique shop when the Italians drove up and blasted a shotgun through his window . . . it was almost too much to bear. They had invaded his life. And it wasn't so much the violence that was unsettling; the racing down the interstate or roughing some guy up in an elevator. That he at least had some control over. It was the being scared. That was becoming a constant.

But it was what it was. There was no time machine. Perhaps there would be no way to square it with these guys except with bloodshed. Blood for peace. As the saying went, like fucking for virginity.

He saw that it was five now so he stood and walked over to turn on the television and hear the sound of the evening news. The bright, colored people came into his living room and spoke of places to go for Valentine's Day. Chicago loves, or some such theme. It was all good cheer, a well-intentioned attempt to help the viewers get through a long cold winter. February fourteenth would come and go and then the next month we'll all get drunk and stamp our feet at the St. Patrick's Day parade. And when the first warm, sunny day comes after that we'll all feel a little bit better. If we're alive.

Maitland wondered, what would a wife say to him now?

He didn't have a wife. He had one once. What would she have said?

She probably wouldn't have said anything. Probably just rolled her eyes and mentally added reason number forty-seven why it was a mistake to have married Evan Maitland.

What would Bianca say?

She already said he had fucked up. That he never should have gone down to Oklahoma in the first place. That he had gotten into this mess because he was restless and immature and a bit twisted and took up this bounty hunting business because he wanted the danger. Well, maybe she had something there. He had been doing bail enforcement off and on since resigning from the police department and usually it was not that harrowing. Typically, he'd track a skipper down in a bar or an arcade or his parents' or girlfriend's. Sometimes they ran, but they almost never resisted. By and large, it was uneventful work. Barry McDermott had been the first one that led to any danger. Perhaps it was what Bianca meant when she told him he had wanted this. This big fucking, violent shitpot of a mess. Like the gambler who's not satisfied until he loses everything. Bianca wouldn't have much pity for him either.

All right, he thought, we know what she said. What would she say now?

She'd probably say —

— probably say:

I love you.
I love you and I want you to know I'm
    here for you.
I love you and I want you to be careful.
I love you and I want you to come home
    alive.

Yeah . . . maybe. If she were Olivia DeHaviland and he was about to cross swords with the Sheriff of Nottingham. Fight on, Sir Robin! Fight on!

Shit.

She'd probably say: *Stop being such a pussy. Fix it.*

If she wouldn't, she should.

He brewed a pot of coffee and threw the old grounds in the kitchen wastebasket. It was full so he took it out to the Dumpster. To get to the Dumpster he had to walk down the fire escape. While he was down there dumping the contents a car pulled into the alley. Maitland turned quickly as his heart pounded and he remembered he'd left his gun in the apartment.

It was Edward, the fat guy who lived on the second floor.

God in heaven. Maitland waved and Edward waved back. Edward parked his car in the garage, got out and walked by Maitland without saying anything else. They were neighbors that didn't really like each other very much and respected the dislike. It was good because Maitland didn't want to have to feel bad about his state of mind now. *Hey, Edward, do you know if I'd been armed I might have shot you through your windshield? Sorry. Kind of jumpy these days. By the way, would you mind moving your*

*mountain bike inside? It's blocking the stairwell
. . . yeah, now would be good.*

Halfway up the third flight Maitland heard the phone ring. He hustled up the rest of the stairs and picked it up on the fourth ring, beating the answering machine.

"Yeah."

"Evan, it's Jay. Sorry, man. I can't find nothing on her. I've checked Illinois Bell, ComEd, People's Energy. No Diane Creasey. No Diane Johnson."

Maitland sighed. "All right, Jay. Thanks for trying."

Maitland finished his coffee. He knew he wouldn't have the concentration to read, so he watched television. Cold and getting dark outside, the perfect evening to sip a beer, smoke a cigarette and watch a good movie.

But there wasn't a decent movie on cable. USA and TBS playing *As Good As It Gets* for the fiftieth time, the networks catering to the short-term memories of the viewers. Maitland switched the television off. He put on his coat, scarf and gloves. He'd walk down to Molly's Tavern for a beer. It was a place he liked with men around his own age or older, telling funny stories about their ex-wives. The manager was a nice Irish girl who let them flirt harmlessly. He went out the front way, avoiding the fire escape and the alley. And when he got through the courtyard and along the street, he felt better about things. The night air was cold and crisp and he even welcomed the idea of the walk itself. He anticipated the hum of voices and laughter and life. It would be a retreat from his thoughts and his dilemma.

He saw the man cross the street and start to walk in his direction. Okay, he thought. It's okay. It's just a man. And the man came closer and Maitland realized it was a black guy. Which was no big deal; Chicago was a big city and if he was going to start edging away from every black man he saw because of the Jamaican posse he just as well should move to Iowa, lie down in a cornfield and die. Still, he kept his eyes on the man as they came closer to each other. The man stared ahead, not making eye contact and Maitland did the same. They came within fifteen feet of each other. Ten, then five. Then they passed each other. And Maitland felt relieved and a tinge of liberal white guilt and he kept going. And then he heard the vehicle approaching and then a squeal of brakes that means a short stop and he felt alarm as he became aware that the vehicle was a van with no windows and before he had time to process it the sliding door was open and two men jumped out and then he was punched in the back by the man that had walked past him, a kidney punch that took his breath away and he collapsed and was half carried, half shoved into the van.

The door slammed shut and the van drove away.

FORTY-THREE

Trevor Jim said, "Check his pockets for weapons. If he has a cell phone, take it from him."

Besides Maitland, there were four men in the van. Trevor Jim, Maurice, and two young Jamaicans. Serious-looking guys. The driver was young and thin, with the wiry strength of a bantamweight boxer. The other guy was bigger with a more tapered build. Maitland would later hear someone call him Kenty.

Kenty and Maurice went hard on Maitland when they first pulled him in, Maurice giving him a couple of good socks to the face and kicking him for good measure and when it was done, Maitland found that his wrists had been duct-taped together. They told him to stay on his behind or he would get his fuckeen head blown off. He put his back against the wall of the van.

The leader said, "Mr. Maitland, do you know who I am?"

"I got a feeling you're Trevor."

"Yes. Jukie tells me you want something from me."

Trevor sat on a milk crate in front of him. Maurice was next to him, holding a large revolver on him. Maitland saw the other guy take a sawed-off shotgun and move to the front passenger seat, keeping the muzzle pointed at him nonetheless. If he pulled the trigger and missed, he'd blow a hole through the walls of the van that a family could crawl through. But he wouldn't miss with a sawed-off shotgun in the close confines of a van.

So this was Trevor Jim. He looked like a normal guy to Maitland. Handsome. Having fun now. *Jukie tells me you want something from me.* While he had guns pointed at Maitland.

Maitland said, "Did he?"

"Yeah. Something about two hundred thousand. Your peace dividend? I want to ask you myself, is there anything else we can do for you?"

"No," Maitland said. "That two hundred should cover it."

Trevor smiled at him. "You pretty brave fellah," Trevor Jim said. "But brave men die too. We all cowards when we die, Mr. Maitland."

Maitland said, "The way Jukie talks, you're the only one that seems to have a beef against me. Yet you come after me with three men besides yourself. Who's the coward?"

Maurice hit Maitland across the brow with the gun. Maitland groaned and fell to his side. As his hands were tied, he hit the other side of his head on the floor of the van. Bing, bong.

He lay there for a moment. The van made a turn. With effort, Maitland sat back up.

Trevor Jim said, "Before it's over, Mr. Maitland, you going to be crying for your mama. Count on it."

"Yeah, whatever," Maitland said. "I understand you guys are into the westerns."

They did not respond.

Maitland said, "Clint Eastwood, Josey Wales and all that stuff. The reason I bring it up is, instead of this torturing and murdering you've got in mind, how about you and I have a face-off. A draw. *Mano a mano.* I'm missing a lung and I've just had the shit knocked out of me. You'd have the advantage."

Trevor Jim said, "A draw, huh? Like, one two three, go?"

"Maybe," Maitland said. "Or we could do it like the French. A duel. We stand back to back and walk twenty paces. You win and you'll be a legend. Trevor the Kid."

Trevor Jim crossed his legs. And Maitland was aware that Trevor Jim had to perform in front of his men.

"Hmmm," Trevor Jim said. "That's something to think about."

"It would at least be interesting," Maitland said.

"Maybe," Trevor Jim said. "But these fellahs need their entertainment too. Besides, Mr. Maitland, you may win such a contest. I understand you no slouch yourself with a gun."

Maitland looked at Trevor for a while. Cold vacant eyes in the dark; you weren't going to persuade them of anything.

Maitland said, "It doesn't have to be like this."

"It does," Trevor Jim said.

Maitland said, "Where is Jukie?"

"We leaving him out of this one," Trevor Jim said.

"You kill him too?"

"No, mon. We don' kill each other."

"Really," Maitland said, risking a smile. For he knew something about gangsters.

Maurice hit him again. Maitland did not wonder whether it had been worth it. He sucked in breath and let it out before he spoke again.

"You killed Barry."

"Of course we killed Barry. He stole from us."

"Stole from you."

"We a family, Maitland. Share the wealth."

"Okay," Maitland said. "And the girl?"

Trevor Jim sighed, showed Maitland he was making him tired and only tired.

"Yes," Trevor Jim said, "we killed the slut and we killed the thief. What's the point in talking about it?"

"We got to talk about something," Maitland said.

"Mr. Maitland," Trevor said, "your moral judgment means this much to me. The police like to say there's no honor among thieves. But there's no honor among the police either and if you don't know that by now you are a bigger fool than I thought. But you think what you want; it means nothing to me. Perhaps your personal sense of superiority will sustain you when you watch your insides being cut out. I doubt it, though. Before that happens, you going to dig your own grave. Oh," Trevor said, "don't have much to say now, huh, b'woy."

He was right about that. Maitland kept quiet and took in his surroundings. The smell of five men closed into cramped quarters. Music drifting back from the front, Bob Dylan saying you got to be serving someone . . . Dylan? Who listened to Dylan anymore? He remembered reading an essay by some guy that argued, vigorously, that Dylan was a fraud. When and where had he read that? It must have been college. It had been a long time ago. Yeah, but it seemed to put guys in the mood to torture victims to death. Maitland found that the music frightened him. Then he realized, no, it's not the music that frightens. It's the atmosphere it seems to cultivate. It reflected the relative calm of these men. They were driving out to the country to rip him apart and yet there was no sense of unease, no palpable anxiety. *It's because they've done it before,* Maitland thought. To them, the initial grab off the street had been the most challenging part of their mission. Now it was just a matter of transporting him to his place of death. Only they weren't just going to kill him. They were going to torture him.

For what purpose? If he were dead, who would he be able to send a message to? They weren't very well going to parade his corpse around, show people what they could do.

No. They would just do it to do it. And if you could not understand why, you had a few things to learn about human nature.

Maitland looked at Maurice. The man

stared back passively. There did not seem to be any immediate sign that he would smack Maitland again. So long as Maitland didn't show any more disrespect. Jesus, the guy was saving it. Like, what's the point of knocking him unconscious now? They'd want him fully alert when they cut him open. Maurice held a .44 Magnum on him. Dirty Harry's gun and didn't he just know it. Goddam hand cannon, would knock his midsection apart then take out a melon-size hole in the rear of the van. Maurice sat quiet and still. Patient, he was.

Trevor Jim, who was observant, said, "Maurice. I think this fellah thinkin' about misbehavin'."

Maurice said, "No." Patronizing Maitland now. Boy, these guys knew how to enjoy themselves.

"Ah, he may," Trevor Jim said. "He's a clever fellah."

Maurice said, "I've seen him before."

Maitland regarded Maurice.

"Yes," Maitland said. "You were in Oklahoma City, weren't you?"

"Yes."

So. He'd seen Maitland before. Did he mean, I've seen him before and I know what he's capable of? Or, did he mean, I've seen him before and he impresses me not at all?

Looking at the man's stone face, it was hard to tell.

"Yes," Trevor Jim said. "I heard about it." Looking at Maitland, Trevor said, "You shot Richard through the door and killed him."

"He was trying to kill me."

"Ah," Trevor said with mock understanding. "Mr. Maitland, you think us to be savages. But did you ever think that you yourself might be an imposter? You speak of us murdering a thief that chases little girls, but you say nothing of Richard."

"What would you have me say?"

"I'd remind you that he is a man. Same as you. Maybe better man. He didn't pretend he was better than you. You act like you a nice guy, but actually, you pretty cold."

"It was self-defense."

"Bredda, it all self-defense."

"No," Maitland said. "There are distinctions."

"Laid down by you, uh?" Trevor Jim laughed. "You remind me of the policemen in my country. They can kill us all they like. Burn down our property, whip us like animals. But we not supposed to fight back. Distinctions, uh."

Well, Maitland thought, wasn't this ironic. Jukie had told him he didn't have the guts to use the violence necessary to deal with their league. Now Trevor Jim was telling him he was just as coldblooded as any of them. They couldn't both be right, could they?

Oh, fuck this guy. He wasn't going to have some rotten gangster lecture him on who deserved to die and when. You started thinking like that in a — well, let's face it — a combat situation like this, you were meat on a hook. *Yes, come to think of it, I do deserve to be tortured to death.* He did not deserve it. He did not deserve to die this way. To die this cold night. If he lived to see the sun come up, maybe he would give it some philosophical whack-off then, though someone would have to persuade him to do it. And if that made him no better than some tribal fuckhead fighting years of war for no apparent purpose other than to outlive another tribe's unregenerate fuckhead, so be it.

The van left the interstate and turned onto a smaller road. Maitland could not tell if they were driving east, west or north. His view of the outside was limited to an angle of the front windshield. Through that window he now saw a narrow road without markings. The road cut through snow-covered bluffs like a trough. Maitland thought they were probably in Wisconsin. Probably heading east, toward Lake Michigan. They had said something about making him dig his own grave. So at least they weren't going to throw him in the lake. He had that going for him. Like that guy in the movie who wakes up relieved from a nightmare about not being prepared for the chemistry exam to find he's being beaten senseless by German guards. Disemboweled and tortured to death, but not drowned.

The van left the road and turned onto a road that was not paved. A dirt road that had been frozen hard, then covered with snow. The skinny black guy drove cautiously, keeping the van on the road.

The van reached a clearing, its lights illuminating trees. The lights cut as the driver shut off the engine.

Maurice said, "Stay where you are."

The two men at the front of the van got out, came around and opened the back doors of the van. The cold air hit Maitland, sparking him. Trevor Jim got out first. Maurice stayed behind Maitland. Maitland got out and they walked out into the clearing.

They formed around him: Kenty in front, holding the shotgun. The skinny driver who looked like he was about nineteen to his right and keeping his back with an automatic. On his left, Maurice holding his extra large revolver. Trevor Jim was behind Maurice, leaning against the van. Maitland tried to ignore the ten-inch knife Trevor had sheathed in a strap around his leg.

Trevor surveyed the setup. It seemed to satisfy him so he pulled a shovel out of the van and threw it at Maitland's feet.

"Dig, bwoy," he said.

Maitland looked at the shovel in the snow. An insult. Dig. Yeah, see it's the new method. We make the victim dig his own grave before we cut him open. Very imaginative. Maitland looked around. They were standing close enough to shoot him but far enough away to dodge should he start swinging the shovel. Yeah, they'd done this before.

Trevor said, "There was a fellah here before, said we should just go ahead and shoot him. We shot him. Through his hand. Then made him dig anyway. You see?"

Maitland looked at Trevor for a long time, the men exchanging something in that moment.

Then Maitland bent over to get the shovel.

That was when the shooting started.

FORTY-FOUR

To put it mildly, the shots startled him.

Maitland pitched over in the snow, tensing, waiting for the hammer-like blows of gunfire to pour into his back. He felt nothing but the pounding of his heart and he looked up to see Kenty lying face down in the ground. He turned his head up to see Maurice firing into the darkness, at a form that had moved to a place he could not see. Then Maurice was running, around the front of the van and gone, and Maitland thought, the shotgun, where is Kenty's shotgun? And he scrambled forward on hands and knees to find it and then he found it and he heard cracks and he turned to fire at Trevor who was firing at him with a pistol. The shotgun blast was for shit, knocking a hole in the side of the van but missing Trevor completely and Trevor was gone, having run around the van into darkness and Maitland racked the slide to take another shot but then was hit full force by the skinny black guy, knocking the breath out of him. The shotgun released its second blast toward the sky, hitting nothing, and

Maitland was on his back with the guy on top of him. The kid was younger and stronger and he had the advantage of surprise. He pulled the shotgun away from Maitland and threw it to the side. Then he started to pound Maitland in the face with his pistol. Or tried to. Maitland held his hands over his face. He didn't know if the guy's gun had jammed or he just preferred to cave people's faces in with guns. It would be academic if the guy kept it up because Maitland was running out of strength. Maitland reached under the man's shirt, grabbed flesh between his thumb and forefinger and twisted almost the length of a clock face. The man shrieked and in that moment Maitland released the skin and used one hand to hold the man's gun hand while he drove the heel of his other hand into the man's nose. And then the guy did let go of the gun and then he was scrambling away as Maitland pointed the pistol at him, seeing that he was going toward the shotgun and Maitland said, "Hey," and pulled the trigger and, yes, the gun was jammed. So Maitland ran himself as the young black reached the shotgun, racked the slide and turned just in time to see Maitland swing the shovel into his face, bashing him into unconsciousness.

Maitland picked up the shotgun, but kept his eyes on the man lying in the snow, not sure about this one.

There were three shots.

Maitland turned around to see Maurice standing behind him, holding that massive revolver. The revolver dropped from Maurice's hand and he pitched face forward into the snow. He was dead, three bullets in his back, one stopping his heart.

Maitland said, "There's still one more."

"I know," Julie said.

FORTY-FIVE

Maitland walked toward her. She had saved his life. Twice. But there wasn't time to talk about it now because there was another man out there and he was armed and vicious and. . . .

Julie said, "We don't have time for that. I've been shot."

"Oh, Jesus —"

"Calm down," she said. "It went through my leg. I can walk. But I'm going to bleed out if we don't get to a hospital. There's no time for an ambulance. We have to go, Evan."

She stood there in her jeans and sweater and overcoat and Maitland noticed the stain on her thigh. Giving him directives in measured tones. Delaying shock, willing panic away from her. Maitland knew he would have to do the same.

"Okay," Maitland said.

He picked up the revolver and the skinny man's pistol and put them in his coat pockets. He kept the shotgun at his side. He put his other arm around Julie and they moved toward the van, Maitland searching the space around them for a man with a gun, keeping his mouth shut while he did it.

He put her in the passenger seat and wrapped his scarf around her leg.

"Keep your hand on top of this," he told her.

Julie said, "You should know." Jesus, being brave.

Maitland got behind the wheel of the van and started it.

"Julie," he said, "I don't know where we are."

"You go down this road and make a right onto the paved road. Then left at the next four-way stop. It'll take us to Kenosha."

He stopped thinking about Trevor Jim when they left the snow-covered dirt road then hammered it toward town.

"There's no back-up?" Maitland said.

"No," she said. "Just me. Oh . . . oh. Your friend Jay called me. He was worried about you. So I drove by your place on my way home. I saw them take you in Chicago. I didn't know this is what they had in mind. I'm sorry, Evan. I didn't know until —"

"Don't apologize to me," he said. "Don't —" He stopped. He had almost said, *don't die on me.*

Maitland said, "Have you got your cell phone?"

"Yeah. My coat pocket . . . No, I'll get it
. . . Here."

Maitland called 911 and told the dispatcher what had happened and where to
find the men responsible. He told them he
was on his way to the hospital. He told them
he couldn't really talk any longer because he
was driving very quickly and he needed to
concentrate. Then he clicked off the
phone. . . .

"God," she said, smiling. "I had to park
my car about a hundred yards away so they
wouldn't see me. Then I had to walk. If you
knew the timing of it, you'd freak."

"Be quiet, Julie."

"No, Evan. We need to talk. We need to
talk about us." She smiled again. "Just kid-
ding. Evan, seriously. Talk to me. I'm afraid
to go to sleep. You understand that, don't
you? Just keep me talking."

"Okay, Julie. I'm sorry."

"What are you sorry for, you dumb
shit?"

"I'm sorry I got you into this. Your job.
Your leg."

"Oh, shut up. I'm not a dilettante. I'm a
police officer."

"I know," Maitland said. "The best I've
ever known."

"Oh, now you're getting maudlin on me.

Don't get maudlin on me."

"Okay, I won't."

"Jesus. I bet you cried during *Lethal Weapon*."

"What?"

"That part where Danny Glover is sitting on his toilet seat with a bomb underneath and he's, he's *holding hands* with Riggs. God. I thought Mel Gibson was going to propose."

"I think that was *Lethal Weapon 2*."

"Oh, I'm sorry. I am so sorry. I need to get them all straight. Maybe they need to get straight. A bigger homo lovefest you won't see on screen. Do you think Mel Gibson's gay?"

"No."

"No, come on. You can tell me. *Road Warrior, Braveheart,* Man Without a Fucking Face. Straight or gay?"

"I think he's an exceptionally attractive man."

She laughed. A shrieking laugh that frightened Maitland because he knew she was hurting.

"Oh, you're funny," she said. "You really are, you know. My husband isn't. He's just not funny. I told him that. Last week, I told him that. Isn't that terrible?"

"Why should it be terrible?"

"Why? You can't tell someone they're not funny. It's like telling them they're bad in bed."

"Have you told him that, too?"

"Oh, yeah."

Maitland said, "Well, fuck him. He had it coming."

She laughed again and touched him on the arm. "Do you get lonely being divorced?" she said. "How is it being alone?"

"I think you'll like it. I like it, for the most part."

"Yeah, I think so too," she said. "Okay . . . okay. We need to get our stories straight. Well, actually, we just have to get one important detail straight. Before I fired the first shots, the guy with the shotgun aimed at you. Okay?"

"Got it."

"And after that, all hell broke loose. We clear?"

"We're clear."

She did not need to explain herself to him. Maitland knew that any decent police officer would have done what she had done. You can yell, "Hands in the air" sometimes and people will drop their guns and everything will be fine. Other times, it's a very bad idea. Had Julie done it a few minutes ago, they would have both been killed. No doubt about it. It was a thing you could only understand if you were there.

Maitland said, "Actually, I heard him say, 'Get ready to die, bwoy.' "

"Really?"

"Yeah. You weren't close enough to hear it. But I did."

She smiled at him. "Bwoy," she said. "That's good."

She closed her eyes, then opened them on Maitland.

"Evan?"

"Yes?"

"Don't look like that," she said. "I'm going to be fine."

He was doing about ninety. But the lights of Kenosha were coming into view. He looked at her for what seemed like a long while. Then he said, "Okay, Julie."

"Okay," she said.

She looked out her window.

Maitland screeched the van into the semicircle in front of the hospital's emergency room. He helped her out of the van. As the doors whooshed open, he said, "Detective Ciskowski, you are remarkable."

"That's what they used to tell me," Julie said.

FORTY-SIX

When he was nine years old, Trevor Jim had seen a policeman shoot a man sitting under a tamarind tree. The man had been unarmed and the policeman laughed when he did it. A boyfriend of his big sister's had been riding in a car that was ambushed by policemen. He got killed too. Supposedly he was a member of the Workers Party of Jamaica, a Communist, and that was reason enough. His name was Lester Thompson. In the first two months of 1985, almost sixty people died from gunshots in Kingston, half of them killed by the police. Lester would take little Trevor to all the good films, particularly the westerns. Trevor memorized colorful scenes, the music and dialogue from the spaghetti westerns. He saw *They Call Me Trinity* with Lester and Lester told him that there was a policeman who took that name for his own. His name was Keith Gardner and he dressed all in black. Keith Gardner was close to the prime minister, Lester said, so he can kill anyone he like. He killed his own wife, Lester said, shot her in cold blood and they don' do nothin' to him. It's what's wrong with our country, Lester said. It's what we need to change.

Trevor liked Lester, but he would come to think that Lester was a fool. A boy. He should have had a gun with him when he was driving that Volkswagen in Spanish Town. He might have died anyway, but at least he would have taken a couple of police murderers with him. Besides, the island was hopeless. Talk of changing things and running out the corrupted powers was a waste of time. Lester said that after they gained independence from Britain they had just substituted it with another group of tyrants. Now it was breddas shooting breddas and it broke Lester's heart. Lester thought the white man could not have planned it better. But Lester was a fool and he stayed. He should have left. He should have come to America.

But the police in America ambushed too. They had certainly ambushed Trevor and his crew tonight. No warning, no shouts of identification. Just shots, and then Kenty was dead. Then Maurice. And Alex was lying there unconscious.

Returning from his hiding place in the woods, Trevor wondered, where did they come from? Where had they gone?

He had come out of the woods to find two

men dead and the van gone. God Almighty, what was he going to do? The van was gone. The ironic prospect of a Jamaican freezing to death in Wisconsin was not lost on him.

He called Jukie on his cell phone.

"Jukie," he said.

"Yeah," Jukie said.

"You know where I am?"

"Yes."

"I need you to come out here. Now."

"What's the matter?"

Trevor did not like to say too much on cell phones, even in the country. Police scanners picked up things. He said, "It's bad. Come right away."

He clicked off the phone.

Alex was stirring now. He was alive.

Trevor Jim walked over and crouched down to speak to him.

He said, "What happened to Maitland?"

"I don't know, mon," Alex said. "He hit me with the shovel. My pistol jammed." Alex looked at Kenty and Maurice. "They dead?"

"Yes," Trevor Jim said. He sighed. "I think the police will be here soon. More police." Trevor stood up.

Alex stared at Trevor then, sensing something awful. He said, "Trevor —"

Trevor Jim shot Alex in the head. Alex fell

over and Trevor put another bullet in his head.

There could be no witnesses. Alex was in no shape to move quickly. The police would find him and take him in for questioning and he would flip. They all flipped, Trevor thought. A bredda had flipped on Lester and another bredda had killed him. To his dying day, Lester had never understood it.

The ER physician looked young enough to be selling magazine subscriptions but he had authority and weight in his voice and he did not hesitate to tell Maitland to get out of the operating room and that his partner would be okay. He backed out and stood in the hall and an administrative nurse told him she had called the police and they would be here any minute to question him. Maitland told her he was in law enforcement himself and left it at that. It was partly true and it seemed to relax her when she heard it.

He thought about the warrior on the operating table, the good soldier that had saved his life and asked if Mel Gibson was a faggot. He told himself that she would be okay. That she had to be okay because if she wasn't, if she had given her life for his, given her life for a furniture salesman that coveted married women and business partners, then something unclean would cling to him forever. He told himself to believe that she would be okay. That she would survive to become happily divorced like him. Don't die on me, Julie. Don't fucking die on me.

Goddam, she had done it. Killed one man in his tracks and then shot another three times as he was about to end Maitland's life.

But who had shot her? Had it been Maurice or Trevor?

"There's still one more," he had said.

And she had answered, "I know."

Trevor Jim was still out there. The skinny young one too, if Maitland hadn't killed him with the shovel.

How would they get back?

They might find Julie's car. Hot wire it and drive it back to Chicago. Or, drive it to the nearest town, dump it and steal another.

If they didn't find the car, what would they do? Where would they go? Would they die of exposure? Would Maitland be so lucky? He knew he would welcome Trevor Jim's death. He did not pretend to feel otherwise.

He could hitchhike. Maybe hitch a ride from one of the many police cars that would swarm the place within an hour. But he's not stupid. Don't presume all crooks are stupid, Maitland had learned. Particularly men like Trevor Jim. He remembered one of the drug task force guys telling him, "The thing about these posse members is they can be quite charming. Good conversationalists. And sharp businessmen. If only they'd have turned it to something positive." Trevor was not dumb. He was not going to stick his thumb out on that rural road.

But it's cold out there and he'd have to get out of there somehow.

Maitland looked at his watch.

The police would be here soon. He would have to tell them he was not actually a police officer and that Julie Ciskowski had not been authorized to tail him out of Chicago and that the whole thing had started with a crooked lawyer that liked to chase underage girls . . . if he were lucky, they might wrap up the preliminary interviews by lunchtime tomorrow. But Trevor Jim would be gone by then. He'll be gone in an hour, Maitland thought.

And with that he found himself walking to the stairs, avoiding the prospect of the elevator doors opening up to reveal blue uniforms. At the first floor he looked through the small window of the stairwell door, watched deputies walk in. They passed by and he walked out to the van. He started it and left.

The call went out over the radio that two men were dead and another two were on the loose. They had shot a Chicago cop and she was in the emergency room. It created a rush for the police officers who responded: two sheriff's cars rushed out immediately and they were later chased by a state patrol vehicle and a Kenosha K-9 unit that was exceeding jurisdiction but had been offered by the night watch. They raced up the road to the scene of the shooting and to join in the manhunt.

The dispatcher said the suspects may be driving a black 1996 Acura 2.5TL that belonged to the police officer they had shot.

The police cars formed a caravan, their own posse, cutting through the rural road, their sirens piercing the cold night air.

Long before he ever heard a siren, Trevor knew that Jukie would not get there in time. He could get upset and start kicking snow but it wouldn't do him any good. He should not have come out here in the first place. He should have let Maurice handle it. Maurice would have tortured Maitland and done a damn fine job of it on his own. But Trevor now had to admit to himself that he had gotten greedy and wanted to partake. He had wanted some too. Stupid, bloody stupid. And now he was stuck out here in the snowy hinterlands while the country cops got closer and closer. If he had stayed in town, he would have been okay. The police would have come to him and asked him what he knew about three of his associates being shot to death in the fields of Wisconsin. Well, two of his associates . . . Maybe it was necessary for him to have come.

Trevor weighed the possibilities. If he stayed and simply surrendered, he could explain it. Or, he could explain nothing. Take the Fifth and say, "I didn't kill them; they are my friends," and say nothing else. What could they prove? If the police were on their way to this remote place it could only be because the bounty hunter had called them. There's your killer. He shot Alex. The police shot the other two. Let Bobby handle it.

Bobby Coyle — his real lawyer. The one he used when the shit threatened to come over his ears. Bobby knew what to do. Not like that fool Barry. Barry was to be used for different purposes. Bobby had referred Trevor to Barry, knowing that Trevor was looking for a way to launder profits, looking for someone to do things Bobby wouldn't do. It had seemed like a smart idea at the time. Trevor wanted Bobby to remain out of the trade, for Trevor's benefit more than anything. He did not want the police to have anything they could use against Bobby because then Bobby might turn on him. Too bloody much. Too many things, too many people to keep straight. Barry had screwed him. And Trevor realized it had not been a personal thing against him; he was in trouble with the law and he wanted traveling money. But Barry was a child. He would get caught eventually and he would eventually flip on Trevor. The bounty hunter had found him in a matter of days. *They* had found him in days, using methods not available to the bounty hunter.

Yeah . . . maybe Bobby could handle it.

But it would be better if the police didn't find him here. He could hear Bobby saying that. *If only you hadn't been there.*

If only you had left it to Maurice.

If only the Italians had killed the bounty hunter earlier.

If only the bounty hunter didn't have someone helping him.

If only Barry hadn't fucked a little girl.

If only.

Trevor walked west, into the trees. He would continue west, keeping parallel with the road they took out here. If he heard a helicopter he would bury himself in the snow and hope the infrared wouldn't detect his body heat underneath. His goal was to reach another road, running perpendicular, call Jukie from there. Hopefully the roads were built on square mile rural grids, so it would only be a matter of time.

The trees thinned out and he found himself in a field. He walked on through the snow. He did not run because there was no need to run. Running was panic and the walking kept his blood warm. He figured he would be at least a mile away before the police arrived there.

He had trudged through a half mile of the field when he heard the sirens. He stopped and listened. To his left. They were coming. He remained still for a moment. Then started walking again. The sounds wailed closer and then he saw the first police car, about a quarter mile to the south going east on the road.

Trevor dropped to the ground.

But their headlights pointed the direction they were going, not out at a field he lay in. He lay in the snow with a feeling that was almost pleasant as three police cars passed and then a fourth.

He stood and began walking again.

★ ★ ★

For a while, Jukie thought about just leaving him out there.

Trevor had only said, "It's bad. Come right away."

What did that mean? How bad? Who got killed? Was Maitland still alive? What did he mean?

Earlier that day, Trevor had told him they would take Maitland out to the country and do it themselves. Telling Jukie he was soft and not up to the job. Jukie smiled at the insult, said, "Go with God, bredda." Would that he had.

Jukie thought it out: if he ignored the call, the police might catch Trevor. If that happened, Jukie would leave town because Trevor might tell the police that Jukie was the one that killed Barry McDermott. Or, Trevor could get killed, shot to death by the police, or freeze. But that was risky. If Trevor lived and got back to Chicago he would want to punish Jukie for his insolence, probably kill him. Trevor did not forgive. Jukie remembered the time Trevor got robbed outside a crackhouse after he left. The robbers let him live but took all his money. Right away, Trevor decided that the people inside had set him up so he went back in and killed everyone there. Everyone.

Four men and they didn't see it coming. He'd done it by himself too.

There was another possibility: if Trevor escaped without Jukie's help, Jukie would have to kill him. A preemptive murder. But, Christ, it would be complicated.

Next to him in the bed, Jukie's woman said, "Where are you going?"

"You don't need to know," Jukie said.

He got up and dressed, took the elevator down to the XJ6 and left.

Maitland saw the flashing cherries up ahead and turned onto the dirt road. He was stopped before he got a hundred yards, spotlight in the windshield, officers yelling at him to show his hands. He followed their instructions and after everyone calmed down, the lead deputy brought him to the clearing and showed him the corpses.

Maitland looked at the skinny one with a bullet hole in his forehead.

Maitland said, "Collins did this."

The deputy said, "Not you?"

"No," Maitland said. "I hit him with a shovel. Detective Ciskowski shot these two." Maitland surveyed the scene. Police cars, deputies and a highway trooper standing around with flashlights, the K-9 dog handler showing the German shepherd what scents to discard and what one to focus on.

"Well, he's gone now," the deputy said. "The dog would have found him if he were around here."

Maitland looked around, got his bearings. Trevor would not have run east because that would have led to Lake Michigan. He would not have gone south because that would have taken him to the road traveled by the patrol cars. So it would be north or west. North or west, north or west. . . .

Maitland said, "Have you got a helicopter?"

"Not in this county," the deputy said. "We don't get many manhunts around here."

"I understand," Maitland said.

"We can call Milwaukee PD; they'd probably send theirs."

Maitland was aware of who he was: an ex-Chicago cop with no jurisdiction here. The deputy looked about thirty, tops, and was being helpful. It was lucky, really, because he could just as easily have been a fifty-year-old hardass and made things difficult. Maitland was careful, letting the deputy know this was his scene and he was in charge.

Maitland said, "If you could. This guy's

pretty smart." He said, "I was thinking because your cars are here that he probably ran that way. Or, that way."

"Yeah," the deputy said. "There'll be patrols on all these roads. I don't think he'll get far."

"Maybe," Maitland said.

A patrol car cruised by, its lights plowing a beam down the road and reflecting off the snowbanks. It passed.

Trevor crawled out of the ditch and dialed Jukie's number on his cell phone.

"Yeah," Jukie said.

"Don't go all the way there," Trevor said. "The police are there. Make a left on Seven Mile Road. Stop at post office box 15301. One five three oh one."

FORTY-SEVEN

One of the officers on the scene made a joke about dead black guys and it struck Maitland as wrong. Not offensive, per se — he didn't have time for that — but wrong. *You're joking, you fuckheads, and this man is going to escape.* It made him upset and some part of him knew he couldn't sit still anymore. He turned to the lead officer.

"I need a car," Maitland said.

The young deputy said, "You can't have a car."

"Lend me one of your men. We'll cruise down these roads. Have a look."

"Evan, we've got patrol cars out there already —"

"Deputy," Maitland said, "this guy tried to kill me. I got lucky tonight. I can't always be lucky." Maitland said, "Please."

The deputy in command sighed, then looked around to see if anyone of higher rank was there to give him grief. There wasn't. He called out to another deputy.

"John," he said. "Take Mr. Maitland back to town." He paused. "Do a perimeter search of the square mile on your way back.

Then radio in, I'll tell you what to do next."

The junior deputy was about twenty-five, young and thick in the shoulders, wearing a crewcut. Deputy John Bush, a cop that looked like a cop. He and Maitland got into the county Chevrolet Impala patrol car and reached the road. Deputy Bush put the needle up to eighty, lights turning.

Maitland said, "John, would you mind not running your lights? I don't want Collins to know we're coming."

Deputy Bush looked at him uncertainly. But he cut the lights.

"You Chicago cop, huh?"

"I'm retired," Maitland said. "You thinking about coming on board?"

"Yeah . . . maybe. My wife doesn't want to live in Chi-town, but the money and the bennies is something I'd like."

Maitland thought about what little influence he had at Chicago. The quickest way for Bush to be eliminated for consideration from the academy would be to say Evan Maitland referred him. A venial sin, deceiving a rural cop. But he needed the man's help.

Maitland said, "You ought to look into DEA. Probably better money there. Better place to work too."

"You got friends there?"

"Yeah. You gonna make a right here?"

"Yeah."

Yeah, guy. He could refer the young cop to Jay Jackson at DEA and Jay would say, what? Maitland referred you to me? For what?

The road they traveled down was unmarked. There were patches of tar and the pavement crumbled off into the ditches on the sides. They passed a propane tank and then half a mile later a sign that said Leonard's Wrecker.

Deputy Bush, "You shoot all three of those guys?"

"No. Detective Julie Ciskowski shot two of them. Collins shot the skinny one."

"Lady cop?"

"Yep," Maitland said. "She shot a guy on a train platform too. In Chicago."

Deputy Bush shook his head, wondering where the catch was.

Maitland leaned forward. He peered out the windshield.

"There," he said. "You see those taillights?"

"Yeah . . . ? They're about a quarter mile away."

"Get up to them."

Bush floored the accelerator.

Maitland said, "Don't turn on the

flashers. I need to see something."

They got closer.

And then closer.

And then close enough for Maitland to see the familiar taillight design of one of the prettiest cars ever made. With a blue and white Illinois tag to match.

"Jaguar XJ6," Maitland said. "That's them. Call it in."

FORTY-EIGHT

Trevor lay in the back seat and he stayed there even when he saw the red and blue flashes invade the interior of the car.

Trevor said, "How many?"

"I cyan tell," Jukie said.

"No," Trevor said. "How many cars?"

"Just one," Jukie said, still looking in the rearview mirror. "What do you want me to do, Trevor?"

Jukie did not want to try to outrun a police car. They were on a road that cut straight north. It would be miles before they could angle over to I-94. There was no place to run. He knew the answer to the question he had posed, but he didn't like it. Trevor thought he was indestructible. But life wasn't like that.

"Pull over," Trevor Jim said. "Don't do nothing until I do something. You hear?"

The Jaguar slowed to a stop, pulling over to the right side of the road.

Deputy Bush shone the spotlight on the Jag. There was a black male sitting in front with both hands on the steering wheel.

332

Bush started to get out and Maitland grabbed his arm.

Maitland said, "He's not alone."

Because they were too far north now. Trevor could not have gotten this far on foot. Jukie had to have picked him up a couple of miles back and just continued north. It was not one of those things you could know with absolute certainty, but you had to know.

Bush used the speakerphone that was rigged to his handset.

"ROLL DOWN THE WINDOW. THEN OPEN THE DRIVER DOOR FROM THE OUTSIDE. DO IT NOW."

Maitland took the shotgun from the standing rack. Bush looked at him and Maitland looked back with a *now's not the time* expression and Bush let it go.

Bush said, "Okay?"

Maitland said, "Yeah."

Bush pulled his service Glock .40 from his side holster, Maitland racked the slide of the shotgun and they opened the doors and got out.

Bush took the handset again. The driver had rolled down the window. But he hadn't done anything else.

"OPEN THE DOOR FROM THE OUTSIDE. NOW."

The man obeyed. He got out and stood,

looking into the glare of the searchlight. Maitland recognized Jukie.

But he can't see me, Maitland thought. He can see the shadow of a man.

Maitland moved forward.

Bush spoke, this time without audio.

"Hands behind your head, hands behind your head! Now get down on the ground! Now, goddammit!" Cop talk, quick and frightened.

Maitland said, firm and steady, "Go ahead, Jukie."

And then Jukie could see him. An outline of the man, recognizing the voice of the man he had shot. Jukie studied him quietly. An outline holding a shotgun.

Then he said to Maitland, "Have you called others?"

In the backseat, Trevor cocked his head. *Why would he ask that?*

Maitland said, "Yeah."

Then he moved forward so Jukie could see him.

"Get on the ground *now!*" Bush said.

And then Maitland saw it. Saw all he needed to see. It was slight but it was perceptible and there was no mistaking it.

What he saw was Jukie look toward the back seat of the Jaguar, tilting his head when he did it.

Jukie got on the ground and Maitland said, "Bush." Bush looked at him, confused, and Maitland gestured for him to stay where he was.

Maitland moved forward, stepping, then stepping again and the passenger side back door opened and Trevor's chest and shoulders were out, the gun in his hand, and Maitland shot him. The shot blew out most of Trevor's shoulder and he grunted and Maitland pumped and shot him in the chest. And Trevor stayed there, a bleeding mass, half of his body still in the car, the other half emptying out into the road.

Bush yelled at Jukie, "Stay where you are, stay where you are!" But Jukie wasn't going anywhere. Bush yelled, "Is he dead? Is he dead?"

"Yeah," Maitland said. "He's dead."

FORTY-NINE

Julie said, "You sure that's what he meant?"

"I'm positive," Maitland said. "He pointed Trevor out for me."

Julie was in her hospital bed. She was still on an IV, but the blood she had lost had been replaced and her insurance company had already conspired with the hospital to have her discharged the day after tomorrow. She had turned off "The View" when Maitland came in and he sat down and told her what happened.

She said, "Why?"

"I don't think it's that complicated," Maitland said. "Jukie's a pragmatist. His lawyer will say he didn't know anything about what went on out in the fields. He wasn't there and we can't very well testify that he was. He just went out there to pick up a friend. He wasn't doing me any favors. He wanted Trevor dead. Maybe he understood that Trevor would have him killed otherwise."

"Or was planning to kill him." Julie said, "So he gave you Trevor. You going to lay down on the Oklahoma City shooting?"

"Fuck, no," Maitland said. "He tried to kill me."

"It's nice that it's over, isn't it?"

Maitland said, "It's not quite over."

Julie said, "What?"

"The money," Maitland said. "The stolen money. I think I know where it is. If I find it, who do I give it to?"

"Give it to me," she said. "I think I've had enough of police work."

"I'll be in touch." Maitland walked over and kissed her on the cheek. "Thank you, again."

An upper middle class home in the suburbs with brick walls and an asphalt type roof. The lawns are well maintained.

The garage door opened and a Toyota Camry backed out.

Tony Burns was in the Camry.

The reverse lights switched off and the Toyota motored away. Before the garage door closed, Maitland saw the Pontiac GrandAm occupying the other half inside. And he knew his suspicions had been on the money. He had seen the Pontiac GrandAm once before. In the parking lot of a coffee shop in Oklahoma City.

He got out of the Monte Carlo and walked straight up to the front door. He rang the doorbell and Diane Creasey answered it.

"Yes?"

Maitland said, "Ms. Creasey?"

"Uh —"

"You are Diane Creasey, aren't you?"

She was wearing sweats and a man's T-shirt. Maitland crudely wondered if Tony Burns had finally been allowed to sleep with her.

"Are you a process server?" she said. She was thinking he had divorce papers.

"No," Maitland said. "I'm a bail enforcement officer." He showed her the badge. "I think you better let me in."

"Why?" She was being tough.

"Because you have a lot of money that doesn't belong to you," Maitland said. "And if you try to keep it, you'll end up dead. Like Barry."

"What are you talking about?"

"I'm talking about the money you took."

"Yeah, whatever. Look, you don't leave, I'm gonna call the police."

"Call 'em," Maitland said. "Let them search this house."

After a moment she said, "Who are you?"

"My name is Maitland. And believe it or not, I'm here to help you."

"Wha—"

"You saw Barry, didn't you?"

"What?"

"You saw Barry, didn't you? After they killed him. Four shots. You saw it, didn't you?"

The woman faltered. She looked away.

"That was not an act of God, Diane. Men killed him. They killed him because he stole money from them. Do you know these men?"

"It's not my business. I don't — I didn't owe Barry anything."

"I don't say you did," Maitland said. "Do you know these men?"

"Barry was a shit," she said. "He didn't care about me. He brought those men to my house. They could have killed me too."

"They will kill you. They found him, they'll find you."

"He owes me."

"What?"

"He owes me that money."

"For what?"

"I don't know," she said. "He just does."

"It didn't belong to him," Maitland said. "They'll kill you for it. If your lawyer friend is here when they show up, they'll kill him too."

Maitland regarded the woman for a moment. Then his expression softened.

He said, "Look, you say Barry mistreated you. I believe it. He was not a nice man. Maybe he did owe you something. But he stole that money. This may sound unusual to you, but that money is cursed. Everyone that's been in possession of it has been killed. It's bloody. You take it and run, they'll find you. And when they do, you'll be sorry that the police didn't find you first. Trust me, it's not something you want to fuck with. Okay?"

Twenty minutes later, Maitland left with the suitcase of cash on the floorboard of his car. He stopped at a Winchell's parking lot and counted it.

$789,000.00.

Wow.

He couldn't wait to get rid of it.

Terry wasn't sure he understood it.

"Maitland? Here?"

The secretary's voice on the intercom told him that indeed it was.

Terry Specht said, "He's not armed, is he?"

He heard the secretary sigh. "No, sir. He's got a suitcase."

Goddam, Terry thought. He wouldn't bring a bomb here, would he? No. Maitland was an asshole. A know-it-all, arrogant jagoff. But he wasn't insane. Still, Terry did not want to face him in his office alone.

So he walked out into the hall to face Maitland. If anything were to start, there would be other police officers around to shoot him.

And there he was, the prick, standing at the reception desk. He was holding a bag.

Terry said, "Something I can do for you?"

"Hey, Terry," Maitland said. "I know you got Ciskowski pulled off the McDermott case. So I thought I'd just turn this evidence over to you."

He set the bag on the ground.

Terry said, "What is it?"

"It's the money McDermott stole from the Raetown Posse. The motive. The reason they chased him down to Oklahoma City. The reason I ran into them."

"You just decide to hand it over now, uh."

"No. I just got it this morning. McDermott's girlfriend had it." Maitland said, "Listen, there's $789,000.00 in here. I think we better have it counted. Officially and placed in evidence so the record will be clear and . . . feelings don't get hurt."

"How come *you* brought it here?"

Maitland fully understood his meaning.

But said, " 'Cause I don't think you would have ever found it. Besides, it doesn't belong to me."

Terry Specht gave him one of his long shitty stares. Then he resigned himself to it.

"I'll get Captain Cason," he said.

They counted it out in front of Captain Cason, Specht, Maitland, and a clerk. Cason acted all friendly, shaking Maitland's hand like he was glad to see him back at the department. The piece of shit. Maitland decided then and there that he would try to talk Julie into filing a complaint of sexual discrimination lawsuit against the both of them, put them on the defensive for a change. When he left, Cason shook his hand and told him he should try to drop by more often. Christ.

FIFTY

Bianca was with a customer when Maitland walked in. She looked at him and he looked at her and they both smiled forgiveness and it was then that he knew he was weak and that he had less control over his life than he thought.

Maitland waited in his office until Bianca made the sale. And then she came back and sat in front of his desk.

Bianca said, "You're looking better now."

"Thanks."

"You all right?"

"Yeah. It's done."

"Yes," she said. "It's done."

Maitland said, "Listen. I've been thinking —"

"I don't want you to leave," Bianca said.

"What?"

"I don't want you to leave. I want us to remain partners."

Maitland said, "I don't want to leave either."

"We're still partners?"

"If that's the way you want it."

"That's the way I want it." Bianca hesi-

343

tated. Then she said, "You know, Evan, I'm not gonna apologize for what I said to you before. I was upset, but I meant what I said. I think you got some issues."

"Well, thank you kindly."

"Your life, what you do, it's not my business. But to some extent, it is my business. Do you understand?"

"I think I understand, Bianca."

"I don't want to run this business by myself. And . . . I need you here."

"All right."

Bianca was quiet for a moment. She smiled at him, but before he could say anything, she spoke again.

"How's your friend?" she said.

"Detective Ciskowski? She's okay."

"Okay? She a superhero. And you don't even say her name. But you not fooling me."

"She's a good shot."

"Yeah?" Bianca said, "I think maybe you are in love with her."

"No," Maitland said. "That's not what I feel. I don't think she feels like that either. It's more like we're soldiers that, you know, fought together."

"Soldier, uh . . . is she pretty?"

"Nope. Ugly as a stump."

"You are a liar. My husband said she is very pretty."

"How would he know?"

"He saw her picture in the paper." Bianca said, "Is she married?"

"Not really. She's getting divorced."

"Then what is the matter?" she said. "She pretty, she smart, she brave. She save your life."

"Well, you can't misinterpret something like that. She didn't do that because she was in love with me. She did it because . . . she did it." Maitland smiled. He said, "What is the matter with you?"

"There is nothing the matter with me. There is something the matter with you."

"You know," Maitland said, "I never understand what the hell you're talking about."

About the Author

James Patrick Hunt was born in Surrey, England, in 1964. He moved with his parents to Ponca City, Oklahoma, in 1972. He graduated from Saint Louis University in 1986 with a bachelor of science in aerospace engineering and from Marquette University Law School in 1992. He presently practices law in Oklahoma City, representing primarily police and firefighter labor unions.

The employees of Thorndike Press hope you have enjoyed this Large Print book. All our Thorndike and Wheeler Large Print titles are designed for easy reading, and all our books are made to last. Other Thorndike Press Large Print books are available at your library, through selected bookstores, or directly from us.

For information about titles, please call:

(800) 223-1244

or visit our Web site at:

www.gale.com/thorndike
www.gale.com/wheeler

To share your comments, please write:

Publisher
Thorndike Press
295 Kennedy Memorial Drive
Waterville, ME   04901

1/13

#2-11

2/13

JUL 1 9 2005